JUDGMENT AT RED CREEK

AN EVANS NOVEL OF THE WEST

LEE COOLEY

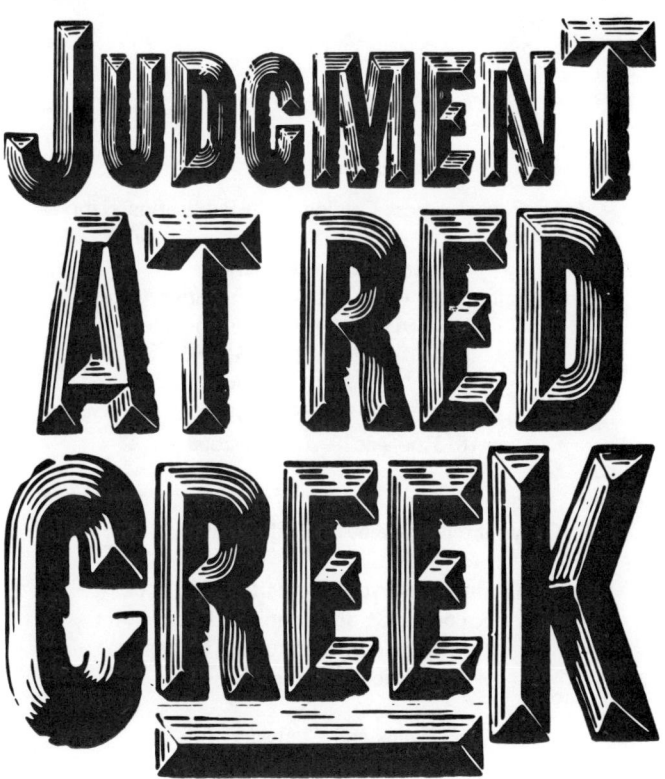

JUDGMENT AT RED CREEK

M. EVANS & COMPANY, INC.   NEW YORK

Library of Congress Cataloging-in-Publication Data

Cooley, Leland Frederick.
Judgment at Red Creek / Leland Frederick Cooley.
p.   cm.—(An Evans novel of the West)
ISBN 0-87131-671-4 : $16.95
I. Title   II. Series.
PS3553.O564J83   1992
813'.54—dc20   92-2668
CIP

M. Evans and Company, Inc.
216 East 49th Street
New York, New York 10017

Manufactured in the United States of America

9 8 7 6 5 4 3 2 1

For my wife, Regina
who put a burr under
my saddle to get this
story told.

Special gratitude is expressed to Michael Pattison, journalist and New Mexico historian, for his maps and descriptions of the old Plaza in Las Vegas circa 1870...

and

...to dear friends, Michael and Susan Robbins, for their loving support and for surrounding us with Napa Valley's incomparable beauty while I completed the final editing on this work in the guest house at their historic Spring Mountain Winery estate, Miravalle, also known to millions around the world as television's Falcon Crest.

L.F.C.

Chapter One

New Mexico Territory 1871

Crouched atop the stone faced earth dam spanning Red Creek, three men, more sensed than seen beneath the black shroud of the moonless night, worked with nervous caution as they placed a heavy charge of black powder in the spillway. Other than the soft chafing of their clothing and the creaking of their heavy leather gun belts, nothing was heard but the familiar medley of night sounds in Red Creek Canyon.

The leader, a heavily built man in his mid-forties, kept a watchful eye on the two gunslinging saddle tramps he had hired in the hotel bar in the pueblo of Las Vegas.

"Don't make no noise now," he cautioned in a gruff whisper as he studied the barely visible shapes of the log and adobe dwellings placed at random along the far bank of the stream.

Reassured when he saw no sign of light in any of the windows, he fastened a long length of fuse to the five pound can of explosive and ordered the men to go ahead of him. Following them, he paid out the fuse carefully until he reached the steep trail leading up to the rim of the broad canyon.

When they had dropped for shelter behind some large sandstone boulders he said, "You keep your fool heads down 'cause I'm gonna light off the powder now. When she blows, them squattin' waterhogs is gonna come a-hellin' out with their lanterns to see what happened. I'm not payin' ya to miss. Drop everything that moves. When I holler, 'Stop shootin,' hightail it up the trail to the horses. I'll be right behind ya. Head fur Tres Dedos like we planned."

When the men found their shelter, he lit a phosphorus match, held it to the fuse until it began to splutter, then scrambled after them.

Braced for the shock, the wait seemed endless. Then, just as the leader began to worry that the fuse had failed, a blinding flash and a head splitting explosion shattered the deep silence. For an instant the afterimage of an angry red fireball lingered in their tightly shut eyes. Air compressed between the canyon's walls surged against them and sent bits of earth and small rocks showering down on them.

Below them, out on the dam, splintered timbers, chunks of compacted earth, and fragmented stone erupted from the structure, seemed to hang suspended for a moment, then rained into the dark torrent that had begun to boil through the breach.

The rolling thunder of the explosion was still echoing in the upper reaches of the canyon when doors burst open. Men and women, most of them in their night clothing, poured out onto the creekside path. Immediately matches flared as lanterns were lit. Holding them high the Red Creek settlers ran toward the dam.

From their cover the three men watched as more people appeared and more lanterns were lit. The slowest to appear were the women and the small children. The leader counted twenty lights as the stunned settlers began to congregate on the dam top. Each light made a perfect target.

"Alright," he barked, "start shootin' and don't let none of 'em git back to the houses fur their rifles!"

The crash of the first volley was answered by open-throated screams of disbelief. A man fell and his lantern tumbled down the stone face of the dam in a cascade of smokey flame. In seconds the dam top became a bedlam as the three men pumped a slanting rain of rifle fire into the panicked settlers.

Men who tried to get to their houses were picked off at their own doorsteps as they ran for their weapons. They fell in the flames of their shattered lanterns. Not an answering shot was directed toward the concealed killers.

A commanding male voice reached them above the screams.

"Put out your lights! Get off the dam! Get back to your houses, quick! Put out your lights! Put out your lights!"

Several lanterns arced into the water. Others were extinguished where they were. Piercing screams of the wounded could be heard above the din of fast-firing rifles. As the last of the lanterns were abandoned or put out, total darkness concealed the carnage. Only the frantic appeals of those struck, and the shouts of others trying to reach them, could be heard above the rush of water and the muted rumble of tumbling cobblestones being dislodged from the stream bed by the rampaging torrent.

No easy targets were visible now. "Lace the place with lead!" the leader shouted. "Shoot at the noise!"

The firing resumed immediately, and new terrified voices were added to the din as random shots found unseen bodies. Moans and the appeals of wounded settlers thrashing in the water were lost as they were washed downstream.

Asa Adams, a disillusioned Confederate captain with Sibley's defeated forces at Glorietta Pass in March of 1862, had been the first on the dam. His had been the first shouted orders to douse the lanterns and get inside. His twenty-six-year-old son, Clayt, still pulling on his shirt as he left his mother and sisters behind, did not hear his father's shocked gasp as he was struck.

Unmindful of his own safety, Clayt ran out along the dam. A rifle slug struck the dirt at his feet. Seconds later he stumbled over Mark Mason. Mason also had served with his father at Glorietta Pass and Apache Canyon. He was on his knees with his face in the dirt. Clayt grasped him under the arms and dragged him off the dam. The thud of impacting lead punctuated the rising chorus of agonized voices as bullets continued to find bodies. Twice, Clayt heard the terrified screams of unseen children.

On the dam again, he found his father's closest friend and fellow Confederate officer, Henry Deyer, carrying his teenage son, Ned.

"Your father's been hit," the older man gasped, "and your sister, Fern. Get to them, for God's sake! I'll help the others—soon as I can."

A few steps on beyond, a lantern had fallen and was still burning. Clayt hesitated, then ran toward it. An instant before he reached to douse it, a bullet smashed into it, spraying him with lamp oil and bits of glass from the shattered chimney. Just beyond he saw a dark shape. Scrambling on his hands and knees, he found Jakob Gruen trying to shield the body of his wife, Hilde, with his own.

"Get her off the dam, Jakob!" The German pewtersmith, who had left New York's Oneida Colony to join with his father and Henry Deyer, reached out and touched his arm. The man's hand was sticky-warm with fresh blood.

"She's gone, Clayt," he sobbed. "She's gone...."

"Are you alright, Jakob?"

"I'm alright. Oh, my God...I'm alright...but Hilde's..."

"Stay down!" Clayt ordered. "Stay down and keep quiet! Those murdering bastards, whoever they are, will shoot at anything, seen or unseen. I'll get back as soon as I can."

The words were hardly spoken when two more slugs ploughed into the spot where the lantern had been. Wheeling, Clayt ran back to the far end of the dam. There he found

Henry Deyer and his eldest son, Oss, bending over Ned. Kneeling close, he saw the wound. A rifle slug had struck Henry's younger son in the lower left belly.

Clayt turned when he heard his younger sister, Nelda's relieved cry.

"Oh, Clayt! Thank God I found you! Fern's been killed and Father's terribly hurt. Oh God, Clayt...come... now..." she pleaded, tugging at his shirt front. "Now!"

A few yards away, just off the dam, he found his mother. She was mute with shock. Dropping beside her, he bent over his father. He was still alive. Next to him lay Fern.

"My God, Clayt," Mary Adams gasped in a horrified whisper, "look at your sister...."

He dropped to his knees, turned her body toward him and bent close. The sight of the wound left him speechless for an instant, then he let out a cry of wordless rage. The bullet had torn away half of her forehead.

In their cover above the dam, in total darkness now, the man who had hired the killers, and who had done much of the killing himself, snapped an order as he saw his men set aside their empty rifles and draw their Colts.

"Save it!" he barked. "We've done good. Let's light out'a here now."

Urging them up the trail ahead of him, he followed the pair to the stand of scrub piñons on the canyon rim. The horses were tethered there. "Mount up," he ordered. "I want us to git back down to the spread before sunup."

"How d'ya know they ain't gonna folla' us?" the younger one of the pair asked.

"Don't you worry none, buster. They ain't gonna be doin' nuthin' down there 'cept diggin' holes fer their dead and fixin' to pack up and git. That's what this here's all about."

He watched them mount then swung into his own saddle.

"Git goin' now. I'll be right behind of ya...in case...."

When they had moved along a few steps he called out, "Wait a second, boys!" As he moved up close behind them he added, "You done such good work, I got a real surprise fer ya."

The two men reined up and turned their horses to face him. In the darkness they didn't see the Colt. An instant later they were both dead, shot through the heart.

An ugly smile contorted the man's face as he pulled the bodies from the saddles and dragged them in the piñon thicket. There he stripped their pockets of the gold coins he had paid them at the bar in Las Vegas, took their guns and belts, their rifles, a throwing knife, and a short-bladed Bowie. When the search revealed nothing more of value he returned to their horses, loosened the reins and prepared to lead them away.

As he remounted he muttered, " 'Be careful about witnesses,' T.K. said." The advice amused him. "Well, I reckon this is about as careful as a feller kin git."

He laughed aloud at his gallows humor and began to ride south to Tres Dedos and Manuel Santos' shabby little adobe rancho.

It was well past midnight when he rousted Santos and his wife, Rosita. The short, squat mestizo appeared rubbing his eyes. Behind him in the doorway, holding a candle and clutching the corner of a blanket for cover, his wife peered out apprehensively.

The man pointed to the riderless animals. "Run them in with yours, Santos, until I come back. And hide the saddles and rifles. Them horses is Kansas branded. If anybody asks ya 'bout 'em, say two strangers come by and paid ya to hold 'em fer a few days. You never seen 'em before. Unnerstan'? *Comprende?*"

Santos tied the rope belt around his pants and nodded.

"Si, Señor. Comprendo."

Pointing to the frightened woman, the man said. "What about her? Kin she keep her yap shut?"

"*Si, Señor.* She weel no talk. *La boca estará cerrada. Por cierto.*"

The man gave them both a threatening look. "If you talk, Santos—or if she talks..." He patted the Colt on his right hip, "it'll be the last time either of you do. *Claro?*"

"*Si, Señor. Claro está.* Nobody weel talk to nobody."

"Good!" He reached into his pocket and removed a ten dollar gold piece.

"Put this in your mouth. It's more'n you've seen in a year. It'll help keep it closed!"

Santos took the coin and clutched it to his bare belly.

"*Muchas gracias, Señor. En el nombre del Dios, no voy a hablar. Es la verdad,*" he said as the man mounted and disappeared in the darkness.

Chapter Two

The first of the sun's rays were slanting over the east wall of Red Creek Canyon when the last of the wounded had been cared for and the thirteen dead had been laid out and covered in the meeting house that now served as an improvised morgue as well as the place where community problems were discussed and Bible readings were conducted by Henry Deyer.

In the Adams house, Mary could not bring herself to believe the horror that confronted them. Clayt and Nelda stood beside her silently praying for the miracle that could not happen.

Henry Deyer's weather-seamed face was a mask, the sort soldiers manage when they are steeling themselves against the sight of comrades killed or maimed in battle. Better than any of them, Henry knew that Asa had been born to inspire confidence and lead. He lifted his eyes and gazed at Clayt and saw in the tall, strong, self-possessed son, the clear reflection of the father and silently thanked God for it.

It had been Asa, then a captain in Confederate Colonel John Baylor's Texas Mounted Rifles, who had urged him to join. Together, they had fought under Baylor when he had routed the Union garrison at Fort Fillmore near El Paso. They had continued then, to drive north to join General Henry Hopkins Sibley's three thousand man army. Asa's company had fought, and how well they had fought!

They had defeated the forces under Sibley's brother-in-law, General Edward R. S. Canby, five miles from Fort Craig on the Rio Grande. Henry remembered the strange unease both he and Asa had felt when the battle was joined. The opposing commanders were married to sisters. There was no more obvious example of the tragedy of Lincoln's "house divided."

Canby had retreated to the fort. Henry recalled the tactical mistake Sibley had made when he decided not to lay siege to his brother-in-law's routed men. Instead, he decided to drive on west to take Albuquerque and Santa Fe. It turned out to be a fatal blunder, largely brought about when Canby had ordered logs, realistically painted to resemble cannons, mounted on the parapets. Having successfully outfoxed his brother-in-law, Canby reinforced Fort Union. The strong point was the key to the conquest of Colorado and the Southwest.

When Sibley heard that Canby was moving on him, he turned to confront the Union troops at Glorietta Pass. When that bloody battle ended in a Confederate rout, Henry remembered Asa's fateful decision to lead his own men eastward to the Pecos Valley. It was on that straggling retreat to Texas that they had found Red Creek. They camped a week there before Asa revealed his proposal that they return for their families and come back to establish a community where they could live out their lives in peace.

As he watched life ebbing from his old comrade in arms, Henry sensed they were witnessing the end of a long shared dream. Hope soared briefly when Asa made a super human effort to force his body half upright.

In a barely audible whisper, he said, "Remember, Henry, when we found this place we swore an end to violence.

Promise me, Henry—and you too, son—not to take the law into your own hands."

When his body sagged, both Clayt and Henry reached out to ease him down. Struggling for one more breath, he forced out the last words he would speak.

"Without the law, there will be no peace in this land...." His head turned slightly toward Clayt. "Promise me, son, that you'll find the ones who did this to our people—find them, make certain of their guilt and bring in the Marshall from Las Vegas. If you don't, there'll be no end...no... end..."

His eyes closed slowly. Then, suddenly, his body convulsed and a moment later they watched in horror as blood welled up in his throat and spilled from his mouth. A moment more and he was gone.

Fighting back tears of rage and grief, Clayt rested a hand on his father's moist forehead, then pulled the cover over his face to conceal the hemorrhage. Mary Adams sank to her knees and buried her face in the bedclothing. Nelda knelt beside her and nestled her cheek in her mother's graying hair. Clayt's face seemed to have turned to stone. Seething with suppressed rage, he wanted to shake his fist at Heaven, scream at a God who would let this happen. He wanted to bolt for his Winchester and his Smith and Wesson handgun, saddle up, and track down the wanton murderers, blow them to bits, slash their bellies and spill their guts as their rifle fire had done to the worst-hit of his people. Instead he lowered his head as Henry, in a strictured voice, intoned a prayer for his battle-tested companion's peace in the Hereafter.

They had scarcely echoed his "Amen" when Oss burst into the room.

"Father!" he shouted, "please come quick. It's Ned!"

Clayt got to the Deyer house first, Oss on his heels. Henry and Nelda were close behind. Ned had been sleeping under a heavy dose of laudanum after a compress apparently had stopped most of the external bleeding. Drenched with perspiration, the youth was delirious now.

Nelda blotted his forehead. "He's blazing hot," she whispered. Henry Deyer pulled down the cover and examined the clean flannel pad. Some blood had seeped through but the glancing rifle slug had not come out the other side. Henry had seen similar wounds after battles. Fever had been a dependable sign of infection, particularly if the gut had been perforated and feces had leaked into the belly cavity. Inevitably, it proved to be a death warrant. Without exception, surgeons refused to operate. The end could come in hours or, more often, after agony-filled days.

Closing his eyes to blank out visions remembered so vividly, battlefield scenes he had witnessed so often with Asa, Henry prayed silently for his younger son's recovery, knowing as his lips moved that he was asking for the impossible.

Four days later the last wagon to make the sorrowful journey moved from the Deyer house. Oss rode beside his father.

Once again, Henry read the graveside service from the worn Bible he had carried into a score of battles. He chose the twenty-eighth Psalm, David's prayer against his enemies. He read it in a voice that betrayed little of his cold desire for revenge.

When he and Oss had committed Ned's body to the rich earth in Red Creek Canyon, he repeated Asa Adams' dying injunction.

"I swear again," he said in a voice flat with cold purpose, "that in the name of God, with no blood of vengeance on our hands, we will hunt down the murderers and, if it's the Almighty's Will, if proved guilty in His sight, we will bring them to justice." He searched the faces before him. "I ask you to pledge again now with your 'amens.'"

A low murmur ran through the ranks of the settlers whose bowed heads concealed eyes newly filled with tears.

That evening, Henry Deyer convened the families in the meeting house.

"There is no power," he began, "that can bring our loved ones back. But there is power in just purpose. We shall use it in the name of justice." He paused and his knuckles whitened as he grasped the edge of the wooden lectern. "Men who can willfully slaughter innocent people are generally hard-drinking men—and boastful. They talk where they drink, in saloons. We don't know where they came from, but chances are they passed through Vegas."

He indicated Clayt and Oss. "The boys have asked to go looking. They leave in the morning to find the Marshall there. Send them off with your blessings. If they happen onto the killers—and from the shell casings there was more than one, most prob'ly two or three—they'll be desperate men. If they get wind of who the boys are, there'll be trouble." He nodded, "For sure. It doesn't seem likely that such men will come back, but you can't tell about the likes of them. So I'm asking for volunteers with rifles and shotguns to stand watch on the dam, and up at the trail head. Each man will stand four hours from sundown to sunup. I'll take the first watch up top." His gaze moved back and forth across the faces.

"I'm asking for help now."

A dozen hands went up. Deliberately, he chose the eldest men. "You younger ones are needed for the heavy work to repair the dam," he explained. "We've got to mend it before storms come in the mountains."

Before him, on the front bench, Mary Adams, Nelda and Jakob Gruen sat with the others, numb and immobile with grief. Clayt and Oss sat by themselves. Both understood the cold, vengeful murder in the older man's heart. It could not be otherwise than it was in their own.

"As for you women," Henry continued, "you can make up refreshments and carry them to the lookouts. Decide among you who will do what and do it quick and quiet." He paused. "That's all, except to ask God's blessings on the boys."

Chapter Three

A clear, red dawn was breaking when Clayt and Oss, followed by Henry Deyer, reached the top of the trail. Henry had insisted on riding that far with them to have a look around.

Suddenly, for no apparent reason, Clayt's horse shied.

"That's funny," he said, "that's never happened before."

Oss pointed to their left. "I think something ran into the brush over there." He reined up and slipped his rifle from the buckskin boot.

"Hold up, son, Henry said as he dismounted. "Let me take a look first." He had moved only a few steps into the thick stand of piñon when he stopped short.

"Boys! Come over here and take a look at this!" A moment later they stood beside him staring down in disbelief at two bodies. Both had been dead long enough for rigor mortis to set in.

"Whoever shot us up must have done this," Henry said. "Maybe these boys surprised them and got killed for it. But on second thought, why would they be comin' our way in the middle of the night?"

Clayt bent down for a better look. One of the men was obviously a half-breed. His body was slim and lean. Stringy, dirt-laden black hair partially covered his pockmarked face. Clayt stepped over him to give the second man a closer look.

He seemed younger, at the most in his early twenties. His hair was light red and his complexion was pale and freckle splashed. His skin bore signs of long exposure to the sun. Unlike the hawk-faced half-breed, the redhead was pudgy with a belly already running to fat.

Henry stooped beside Clayt and picked up the half-breed's stiffening hand. "He's no cowhand. Neither is this fatty," he added, feeling the palm. "These men are saddle tramps and gunslingers. The territory's full of them."

He straightened. "They're the sort who could do what was done to us. No question about that. But the real question is, who killed them and why?"

"More than two men did the shooting, Father," Oss said. "I gathered up Henry casings and Winchester casings. There were a whole slew of them."

During the speculation, Clayt was going through the men's pockets.

"They've been stripped clean," he said, "guns, belts, money, knives. Somewhere around there'll be two branded horses on the loose. If we run across them, that may tell us something."

Henry Deyer pushed one of the bodies with his boot.

"I think we've been told something already. My guess is they were killed by somebody they knew. The signs say they were dragged here and stripped and left for the buzzards. They're beginning to stink already."

He wrinkled his nose. "You boys ride on now. I'll go down and bring up a couple of men to help bury them. There'll be a wheel of buzzards over them by noon. When we finish, I'll look around for tracks and see if they say anything."

He returned their nods and watched as they rode off at an easy lope to the northeast in the direction of the old Santa Fe Trail and the growing pueblo of Las Vegas.

Three hours of riding brought Clayt and Oss to the west bank of the Gallinas River, a small stream that flowed into

15

the Pecos a few miles south of the Gavilan spread. They followed it into town and turned left to the plaza.

It was little more than a crude rectangle of packed earth that had been roughed out in the 1830s. A half dozen buildings were scattered around it. Two of them at the south end were hotels. A saloon and dance hall adjoined the Exchange Hotel. On the west side of the plaza, a few doors north of the American Hotel, a sign read, DICE APARTMENTS.

Clayt and Oss rode along until they came to a sign identifying the stage stop. As they were tying to the rail an old man lounging in a barrel chair out front called to them, "They ain't no stage in today, boys."

Clayt stepped over to him. "We're looking for the United States Marshall. Can you tell us where to find him?"

"I shore kin," the old fellow replied. "You'll find him six feet under. Got himself kilt over on the Conchas a week back, tryin' t'round up rustlers workin' the Goodnight-Lovin' Trail."

Oss joined Clayt. "Has a new one been appointed yet?"

"Nope, Sonny," he replied, deliberately exploring a wiry tangle of gray beard, "an' they ain't gonna be no law here fur quite a spell—though I did hear tell from the stage driver that a new man an' a couple 'a dep'ties is comin' over from Santa Fe next month."

Clayt frowned and moved closer. "Are you saying there's no law at all in Las Vegas now?"

"That's what I'm sayin', mister, 'cept fur the no 'count constable that ain't never here if they's local trouble."

He pushed himself upright and resettled his weather-wilted felt hat. "You boys needin' the law?"

"Could be," Clayt replied.

Interest kindled in the man's rheumy old eyes.

"Sure 'nuff? What happened?"

Clayt ignored the question. "I expect a man like you would know about most everything that goes on here."

" 'Spect I do, mostly."

"Have you see any strangers in town lately?"

"Well now, mister, that depends. What kind of strangers?"

Clayt concealed his annoyance. "Outsiders...cow hands ...saddle tramps...anybody new."

Anxious to prolong a rare opportunity for conversation, the old man scratched his cheek and pretended to think.

"Well now, seems I do call t'mind two boys come in from Kansas some days back." He broke off and frowned. "An' before them, a lone fella rode in. He put up at the 'merican Hotel an' got some new duds. Went out the next day."

"Did you find out who he was?"

"Nope. Never seen him before. None of my concern anyways."

"What about the Kansas boys?"

"Trail dusters. Never seen 'em before, neither. They put up at the hotel, too. Second day they was there that same fella come back. He put up one night and the next day all three of 'em rode south together."

"Any idea where they were heading?"

"Nope. Didn't talk to 'em. Jes' rode right on by. It don't bother me none. I work the stage two days—one day comin' an' t'uther goin'." He brightened. "My real job's guardin' the safe here in the 'spress office." He indicated an old shotgun leaning against the wall beside him. "I sleep in the back, but so fur nuthin's happened." He chuckled. "I guess this 'dobe heap's too small fur the likes of th' Youngers."

Managing a wistful expression, he added, "Sometimes I sorta wish sumpthin' would happen. Then mebbe folks wouldn't walk right on past without even seein' me."

Clayt gave him a reassuring smile. "I'll tell you one thing, my friend, we're real glad we didn't walk by you. Thank you for talking with us." He took a step and turned back.

"By the way, would you remember what those two riders looked like—the ones you say rode in from Kansas?"

"Glad to oblige, mister. I didn't talk to 'em, like I said, but I heard one of 'em say when he rode by, 'This place ain't no Dodge City.' Never bin there myself but from what I hear tell, that's where the Devil goes to practice up on bein' orn'ry."

"But you really didn't get a good look at them. Is that it?"

"Oh, I seen 'em clear 'nuf. Took one t'be injun lookin' and the other one was sorta young...red haired...light skinned...tubby, runnin' t' belly. Neither of 'em looked like they'd of knowed a day's work if they was standin' in the middle of it."

Clayt and Oss thanked the old man, remounted, reined their horses left, and rode south down the plaza. The weathered, poorly painted sign read, AMERICAN HOTEL.

"Let's put up here for the night," Clayt said. "We'll get some grub and talk to the bartender. Remember what your father said about the kind of men who talk in saloons?"

"Sounds like these birds might," Oss agreed.

They paid fifty cents for a poor excuse of a room, washed in the grimy basin, and went in to eat.

The bartender studied them curiously when they took a table. "Howdy," he said. "If yer settin' I guess yer eatin'?"

"We'd like some supper...and some breakfast in the morning," Clayt said.

The man nodded. "T'night it's pork chops, fries, and sauerkraut."

Later, Oss regarded his plate with grim displeasure. "Beats all get-out what a fellow can get outside of if he's hungry enough."

Clayt's chuckle was mirthless. "Please God, I'll never be hungry enough to eat here again!"

The coffee the bartender brought proved to be a muddy mix of chicory and stale army-post beans. It was filled with grounds.

"D'ya figger to set and drink a while before ya turn in?"

"Not tonight," Clayt replied. "We've got a lot of trail time."

"Oh? Where'd you ride in from?"

"Down valley."

The bartender pushed an annoying moustache hair from the corner of his mouth. "Wouldn't be part of the new Gavilan outfit, would ya?"

"No," Clayt answered. "Didn't know the old place was still running cattle."

"They will be. New owners. New super and new foreman. If you're lookin', they're hirin.' "

Clayt nudged Oss's leg under the table. "Could be interesting."

"Foreman's a man name of Harmer. New to these parts. He was in sometime back. Come in ag'in a few days past an' hired two boys that was stayin' here. Next day they all rode out." He laughed. "An' I'll be damned if he didn't come back a couple of days ago. Musta had a real good payday 'cause he come in to the bar carryin' a new silver-mounted saddle. He even took the thing into the room to sleep with it."

He laughed and shook his head in wonder. "He was sure all Sunday-go-t'-meetin' gussied up. Figgered he musta stopped in t'see Inez. She's our fancy lady. A buck a throw, an' worth it too...." He cleared his throat apologetically. "At least so they tell me. I git all mine at home."

"What about the boys who stayed here? Harmer must have hired them."

The bartender nodded. "That's what he done alright, done it right here in the bar. Bought 'em drinks, then give twenty in gold against forty dollars a month. Top pay, I'd say."

He wiped his hands on a dirty apron. "They didn't drop a penny of it. Harmer even stood their grub and room."

"I wonder," Clayt said, "if you remember what they looked like?"

Apparently reluctant to reply, the man shrugged. "Ord'

nary, I'd say. Somebody you're lookin' fur?''

"Not especially. Just curious.''

Relieved, the bartender relaxed. "One was a half-breed. Th'other wasn't much more'n a kid—pale skin, mess of red hair, runnin' t'fat. Wore his rig under his belly. The skinny one wore a bandoleer... 'bout half full. Didn't see the make of the rifle.'' He turned as two men entered and stood at the end of the bar. Clayt and Oss assumed they were regulars. The bartender acknowledged them with a nod, set out a bottle and glasses, and returned immediately.

"The three of them done more drinkin' than talkin', 'specially after this Harmer fella started standing them my best two-bit bourbon.''

"I couldn't pick up too much without buttin' in, but from what I could hear, they were talkin' cows. From the looks of the pair, I figgered he was hirin' them on as outriders guardin' aginst rustlers. Thousand-head herds are on the trail. With new spreads startin' up, it'll git worse before it gits better.''

He turned to look as another man entered. Moving away, he said, "That'll be four bits fur the grub, boys. See ya in the mornin.' ''

When the bedroom door was locked, Clayt eased onto a rickety chair and pulled off his boots. Keeping his voice low he said, "We're as good as sure now. All we've got to do is prove it. With the Gavilan in new hands I can guess what's behind it.''

"Water?'' Oss asked.

"For sure. With thousand-head herds trailing up every good stream in the territory, that's got to be it.''

"Good God, Clayt, they can't drink the rivers dry!''

"In the middle of summer—and that's when they'll be driving—a lot of those rivers aren't rivers for a couple or three months,'' Clayt replied. "Let's turn in. I want to get a sunup start.''

Oss tested his side of an old iron bed that had tormented a thousand bodies. "If supper was any sample, I'm for skipping breakfast."

On the ride back to Red Creek, Oss studied Clayt with a troubled look. Seldom demonstrative ever since the fever had taken his childhood sweetheart and intended bride, eighteen-year-old Hazel Coates, two years earlier, Clayt seemed unusually quiet now. Hazel's death had left a lingering trace of sadness in his eyes and had touched with grimness the lines around his strong mouth that once had so easily broken into an engaging smile.

They rode side by side in silence for a time, then Oss could no longer contain his curiosity.

"You sure look like you're chewing on something, Clayt. Care to talk a little?"

"Nope. I want to ponder on it first," he replied. "I think maybe I've got an idea that'll work."

It was just past midday when they turned their horses into the corral and followed the men over to the meeting house. In less than five minutes Clayt and Oss gave Henry Deyer and the others a full account. When they finished Henry braced an arm on the back of the bench and frowned thoughtfully.

"You've flushed them out alright," he said, "but we can't go riding down there and accuse this man Harmer and whoever he takes orders from. There's no doubt he shot those two men without a chance, probably because he knew he couldn't trust them as far as he could throw a steer uphill."

John Bates glanced at Jakob Gruen who had been working beyond his capacity to contain his grief. "Jakob and I have been thinking too," he said. "Even if we get proof, what can we do against the likes of them, what with the marshall dead?"

"It's a problem," Clayt agreed, "but suppose we find a

way to get proof first, then figure the best way to get it to the law.''

Henry was skeptical. "How do you figure on just getting the evidence?''

"Before I tell you,'' Clayt replied, "I want you to know that I don't want to hear any arguments. Unless you shoot me in my tracks, I'm going to try it.''

Henry seemed about to protest but Clayt's grim, set mouth made him pause. "Well, get it said. After we hear it we'll figure out whether to back you or pray for you.''

"First off,'' Clayt began, "we know they're hiring at the Gavilan. If I show up, they won't know me from Adam's off ox. I'm just a stranger looking to hire on somewhere. I'm a buff hunter for the railroads. With the herds cut to ribbons now, I'm out of work.'' He paused half expecting some reaction. None came as the men listened in silence.

"I'm going to ride in and make it easy for Harmer to put on a new hand. Once on, I'll work and listen. When I've got enough to stand up with the law—if I do—then I'll drift on south, circle around, just in case, and get back here. Then we can figure out the best way to use what I've found out.''

He paused again, and again there was no reaction. Henry and the others seemed to be assessing his chances for success.

"We've got to get the goods on Harmer and whoever gives him his orders. That's the first thing. If we don't do that, and follow father's advice, than all we can do is wait for more of the same.'' He looked at each man in turn. "If we wait for that, we might as well pack up and move on—and if we do that, they win and we'll lose and keep on losing. That's the size of it, no matter how we look at it.''

Oss couldn't believe his ears. "Good God, Clayt! No wonder you didn't want to tell me what you were chewing on! Are you loco? You'll be dead the first day. You're no cowhand!''

On his feet, he thrust out a threatening finger.

22

"You don't want any back talk? Well, Clayton Adams, you just wait and see what you're going to get from your mother and Nelda when you bust out this hornet's nest! Your Dad gone. Fern gone, and you a likely next. What right have you got to think that you won't get flushed out and killed, too?"

Henry Deyer rose and rested a hand on Oss' shoulder. He had known Clayt since his early teens. He had never met a more modest, self-possessed, and confident lad. From the time he had learned to handle a repeating rifle, Clayt had been the best game hunter in the party as their wagon train made its way north along the Pecos from Texas. Clayt had ridden point with him. He was a born scout. When he got his Smith and Wesson forty-four, he practiced drawing until he was much better than just good. Several of the men had said to Asa, "That boy of yours is a natural. Let's hope he don't get too all-fired handy with it." Asa knew his son and he had no cause to worry. Clayt may have been born to guns but he was no compulsive killer.

When Oss seemed about to berate Clayt again, Henry took him by the arm. "Cool down now, boy. Clayt's making the only sense there is. I don't expect those mad coyotes are going to come down here and ask if we've had enough. They'll be back again when the dam's fixed, but one thing's for sure: They won't surprise us twice!" Urging Oss to follow him, he added, "Let's have no more talk now."

At the midday meal Clayt's decision brought wails of protest.

"You're head of the family now," his mother pleaded. "If anything happens to you there's only Henry and Oss and Nelda. Fourteen are dead. Mike Nathanson and Thad Jones are just barely hanging on. Five others are only able to work part time. I'd rather walk away from all of this than face the chance of you getting hurt. Half the families are sick to death and frightened. If you didn't come back, they'd pack up and leave. That would be the end of your father's dream!''

Clayt spoke gently. "Leave for where?''

"I'm a school teacher, Clayt. I taught all three of you. I can still teach . . . in Texas . . . or even back where we came from originally, in the Carolinas. There's still family there.''

Nelda got up and came around behind Clayt. Circling his neck she pulled his head back close to her.

"Don't do it, Clayt. I know how you feel with father gone. You don't care about danger anymore. That's how we know you felt when Hazel Coates died. We watched you and prayed that someday you'd see that one of the other girls could love you.''

Smoothing his thick dark hair she pleaded, "It's foolish, Clayt. Let's just go on with our lives. I know father would have wanted it that way.''

Clayt reached up with both hands and loosened his sister's embrace. Rising from the chair, he said, "We aren't going to bring the dead back to life. We can't stop living. And I can't go on living in peace with myself if I don't do what I know Father would have really wanted. We've got to get proof and find a way to bring the guilty parties to the law.''

He gazed at his mother and sister, and spoke gently.

"I promised father, and I promise you, on his grave,'' he said, "that I'll be alright—and I'll be back. Count on it.''

He moved around the table to his mother. Leaning down he kissed the top of her head. The overt show of affection brought on new tears.

"Don't pester me any more now,'' he said quietly. "Just keep me in your prayers.''

Before he retired, Clayt put together his saddle roll. It contained blankets, extra clothing, spare boots, and oil-skins. The single-action forty-four was snugged in its holster with the full ammunition belt. He packed it in his saddle bag. The

Winchester repeater with a full magazine was eased into the deerskin saddle boot. In the left bag he stored jerked venison strips, a razor sharp Bowie knife, matches, small personal care items, and several boxes of spare ammunition.

"I'm as ready as I'll ever be," he said half aloud, as he undressed and turned in.

Chapter Four

The Red Creek settlement was dark except for a light in the Deyer cabin when Clayt checked his saddlebags and bedroll one last time and mounted. In his haste to get an early start and avoid more pleading, he did not notice that one of the horses was missing from the dozen saddle-broke work horses kept in the corral.

On the far side of the dam, he turned his mount downstream a hundred yards to the small cemetery. He dismounted, dropped the reins, and walked along the fourteen newly mounded graves, pausing at the last three which held his father, his sister, and Oss's young brother, Ned. He stood longest at his father's grave and silently reconfirmed his promise. Crosses had not yet been made to identify the victims. On the way along the rows he had passed the grave of Hazel Coates. He had loved her since she was fifteen and he was eighteen. Three years ago, almost overnight it seemed, tick fever had taken her. Standing as he did now, he could still feel the pervasive emptiness that displaced the quiet eagerness that once had given the promise of new meaning to his life. Their marriage was also a part of the dream.

Mounted again, he reached the top of the trail just as the sun was slanting over the long grassy rise that marked the edge of the high plains to the east.

Suddenly, from behind a stand of piñons, Oss appeared mounted on his horse. Clayt let out a surprised grunt.

"What kind of damned foolishness are you up to?"

"I'm going to ride with you for a way."

"You're going to do no such thing! This is my show. I'm riding alone, Oss. Now turn that nag around and get back down there. Your best job is to keep Mom and Nelda quieted down."

"That'll be like telling the sun to stand still."

"Well, try anyway!"

Oss threw up his hands. "I'll promise you one thing, Clayt, if you're not back in a reasonable time, I'll be riding out to look for you."

"And that's something else you're not going to do," Clayt snapped. "I love you like a kid brother but if you get too stiff-necked I'll take you by the scruff and the seat of your britches and fetch you back myself. This is my show. I'm looking for work, not trouble. If you come riding in, you'll get us both shot. You saw what those people can do. Now get on back down there. I promised Mom and Nelda I'd be back. I promise you that, too. And you'd better promise me you'll not come riding down to Gavilan like a one Indian war party. We don't know what kind of hands Harmer has down there, but we know what kind two of them were. Now get on back down, Oss. I'm going to be just fine. I've got my whole story set."

Oss remounted and watched glumly as Clayt rode away and disappeared in the lingering predawn gloom.

Clayt reached the trail intersection in a little over an hour and headed south. Another hour and a half brought him to the Santos ranch. It was no more than a shabby collection of sagging sheds, a corral, and a weather-eroded one room adobe.

As he neared the place, two men who were leading a pair of horses toward the corral gate, stopped. After a few words, they turned quickly and led them out of sight.

Clayt tied up at the hitching rail next to a lone saddled animal. As he dismounted the ornaments on the saddle caught his eye. Without appearing to, he noted the details of both the saddle and the bridle. They were new and heavily ornamented with silver.

He recalled the bartender's comment. The outfit most probably was Harmer's. He had intended to ride on through but now, with what could be a stroke of good luck, he decided to pretend to be stopping for coffee.

Rosita Santos, a heavy, once pretty girl, was holding the tattered burlap drape aside. Raising his hat, Clayt said, *"Buenos dias, Señora. Yo quiero comprar café. Es possible?"*

Before the woman could answer, a scowling, heavy-set man appeared from around the corner.

"Who are ya, and who are ya lookin' fur?" he demanded. Struggling to conceal his anger, Clayt replied in an even voice, "My name's Clayton. In Las Vegas I heard about possible work on a new spread down-valley."

Jake Harmer did not miss a detail of the stranger's dress or his mount. The animal did not have the wiry look of one that had done much range work. Neither did the man himself.

After a deliberately prolonged silence, he said, "What kinda work do ya do?"

"Whatever needs to be done. I've been buff hunting. Not much doing now, with the government and railroads mostly buying beef. I've done some wrangling and trail riding—and some smithing and carpentering."

As Clayt spoke, not the rough argot of the typical cowhand or plainsman, suspicion narrowed Harmer's eyes still more.

"Where ya from, Clayton?"

"I told you. I came from Vegas."

"Before that!" he snapped. "Where was ya born?"

Clayt managed a patient smile. "I was born in an old

Murphy wagon on the trail west of Independence. My father was a preacher from Virginia. My mother was a schoolmarm. We got as far as Council Grove and my father died. We turned back to St. Louis. I got some schooling there. Six years ago I started working my way west.'' He shrugged and deliberately broadened his smile. "Now you know all there is to tell."

Jake Harmer continued to study the newcomer. A schoolmarm for a mother would explain the fellow's manner of speaking—except that it sounded a bit more south, somehow.

"Can you handle a six-gun?"

"Depends. I favor my Winchester," he replied, indicating the rifle in the saddle boot.

"Can you rope and bust out a bronc?"

"If I have to." Clayt was about to say that he had broken the mount he was riding when he realized with a start that the man who had to be Jake Harmer was looking at the Red Creek brand.

"I'd sure like to bust out one of my own soon," he said, hoping his improvised story would hold water. "My horse went lame a couple of days back. I borrowed this one from some settlers at a place called Red Creek. Met two of them on the trail and went down there with them. Left twenty dollars in good faith. I'll take this nag back as soon as I can." He managed a humorless grin. "Lame or not, they still got the best of the bargain."

Harmer's fixed gaze relaxed a bit. He reached for a plug of black tobacco and bit off a corner. Clayt waited until he had settled the quid in his unshaven cheek, then with a convincing show of respectful affability, he said, "Can I ask your name?"

Harmer returned the plug to his pocket. "Name's Harmer. Jake Harmer. I'm foreman of the new Gavilan spread down at Mesa Roja." He spat and the impact raised a small explosion of dust. "I'm takin' two horses from here to add to our string. You lead one and ride with me," he said. "I'm short-handed. I'll talk to T.K. Oakley about puttin' ya on. He's the new sup'rintendent."

The muscles in Clayt's middle relaxed. "Be obliged," he said.

He forced down a half mug of near undrinkable coffee. Harmer sucked a big swig of pulque out of a bottle on the table and wiped his mouth on the back of his hand. He put two nickels on the table. "I'll stand for this. Let's go."

The ride with the extra horses on lead passed with little talk. Clayt's careful attempts to draw Harmer out were not successful. What information the man imparted was useless. It concerned general plans for a half-million-acre spread. When Clayt observed that a ten-thousand-head start-up herd would need a lot of gramma grass and water, Harmer agreed. "In the dry season, it's gonna take every damned drop from the Pecos and everything that drains into it."

"Those settlers in Red Creek seemed to have good water," Clayt said.

"Not now they don't," Harmer replied with a mirthless smile. "We blew up their dam and shot 'em up a little. They won't be stealin' more water now."

So there it was! Clayt's jaw muscles corded as he fought to control his outrage. When he could manage himself he said, "Seem like there'd be enough water for everybody...if nobody hogs it."

"The hell there is!" Harmer growled, turning in his saddle to give him another of his periodic scrutinies. "Them sodbusters in Red Crick got no claim to land or irrigatin' water. The Gavilan's owners got preemtion rights on territorial land and all the water, too. There's gonna be no room for water thieves on any live stream when our herds are built up. That's what we're gonna git inta their dumb heads!"

Harmer was lying. Clayt was certain the cattle syndicates had no intention of paying the government a dollar fifty an acre for the thousands of acres of federal land they would need, even though payment was necessary under the Preemption Act. The Homestead Act was another thing. The government could enforce it. That's why, three years ago, his father and Henry had filed and paid the fees after Congress passed the bill over Southern opposition. All the settlers had chipped in. The land was owned in common, or would be when it was patented in two more years. The simple truth was, the cattlemen would be the illegal squatters and would get away with it because there was no way to stop them.

It was midafternoon when they rode into the Gavilan ranch headquarters and turned their mounts loose in the corral. Harmer pointed to a small adobe. ''Put yer stuff away and come over to the house.'' He indicated a large U-shaped tile-roofed adobe on which a recent addition had been made. It stood in the shade of a stand of old sycamore trees.

Clayt beat the dust from his clothes and washed as best he could in the watering trough. When he approached, Harmer was standing on the porch talking to a tall, middle-aged man dressed in a well-cut, black broadcloth suit. A blue silk cravat was secured around a clean white collar. As he came closer Clayt could see the man was graying at the temples but his obsidian eyes, his heavy eyebrows, and his handlebar moustache were as jet black as his full head of coarse, straight hair.

Clayt stopped by the stairs and waited. Harmer glanced at him but made no effort to introduce him. Instead he jabbed a thumb in his direction.

''This fella calls himself Clayton. He's lookin' fur work. We're still short. I kin use him if you say so.''

Clayt held his breath while Oakley gave him an impersonal sizing up. He hoped he would not be asked any questions.

It was a lot easier to remember the truth. Lies made slip-ups likely. He felt no real uneasiness about making up a story. In this case, he thought, God Himself would have agreed that the end justified the means.

Finally Oakley turned away. "Put him on and try him out."

As Oakley turned to go inside, Clayt caught a glimpse of a young woman moving through an inner room. Probably Oakley's daughter, he thought.

Harmer joined him and pointed to the bunk house about fifty yards away. "Git on over there and ask Buck Tanner to show you where to put yer bedroll." As Clayt started to move away, Harmer stopped him.

"Say—you got a first name, ain't ya?"

"They call me Clay," he replied, deliberately leaving off the T.

Harmer nodded. "Alright. See Buck, then git over to the cookhouse and git some grub. Chow's down reg'lar at sunup. Ya git a half hour fur it."

Buck Tanner, graying, square built and a bit paunchy, was the sort his father characterized as having a "born friendly face." The old professional welcomed Clayt warmly. While he was putting his things in order on the bunk, and in the old wooden box nailed to the wall that served as a storage shelf, Buck Tanner explained his position at the Gavilan.

"Don't know what to expect now," he said, "what with the new owners and all, but I've still got good days left in me, even if it's only workin' as tallyman. We'll see, but I used to be trail boss fur the old owners. Drove many a better'n six-hundred-head herd north to the railroad." He shrugged.

"I guess I'll be alright. I don't cotton up to Harmer or Oakley, but I never seen a man yet I couldn't git along with if it put beans in my pot."

Later, in the cookshack, munching on stringy beef and tortillas that Tanner told him he could expect "real reg'lar-like," Clayt did some more listening. When he finished he settled back.

"What do you know about Harmer?" he asked.

Buck Tanner probed his ear with a forefinger, examined the result, and cocked his head dubiously.

"You'll only know what he cares to tell ya. Let's go back and set on the bunks for a spell. I'll tell ya what I know."

Settled in the bunk house again, Tanner glanced around and moved closer. "He only talks when he's had a few snorts. One of his fav'rite occ'pations."

Clayt remembered the long draught the man took out of the common pulque bottle at Santos' place.

"Oakley brung him up from Texas. He claims he rode with that wild-eyed, murderin' son-of-the-Devil school teacher, Bill Quantrill and his Confederate guerillas at Lawrence, Kansas. That's where they shot up a hundred and fifty men, women, and children jus' fur the hell of it, and then wrecked the town.

"Jake claims Jesse and Frank James and Cole Younger rode with him. He sez he was in the outfit when Quantrill finally got his from the Federal troops in Kentucky in May of Sixty-five."

Buck Tanner explored his ear again. "I'll tell ya one thing, Clay, if Jake's got an ounce of the milk 'a human kindness in him, it's long since clabbered."

"He must be a good man with cows," Clayt said.

Tanner nodded his agreement. "He's that 'right enough, otherwise Oakley wouldn't have brung him up."

"What about Oakley?"

"No man t'cross. Don't trust him, son. He come up from Texas, too—six months back. El Paso. Word is, he bossed a half million acre spread around Big Spring. His ma was half Choctaw, makin' him a quarter-breed. He don't talk much, but the word is that Charlie Goodnight himself calls him one of the savviest cattlemen around. I kin believe it. Guess the Chicago and English owners agree. Word is, he gits a good payday, and an overwrite of a dime a head on every head he delivers to the railroad in good shape. Harmer's his man, an' from the way ole Jake's been spendin' lately, I'd say he's gittin' a good payday, too.''

Buck frowned. "Only thing I can't figger out—Oakley's bone dry. He'd kill a guy caught drinkin' on a drive. But he puts up with Harmer. 'Coarse, s'fur as I know, he only drinks at night.'' He chuckled. "One thing's fur sure, Clay, ya didn't hire on to no Sunday school picnic! With Quantrill fur a teacher, ole Jake's already made his deal with the Devil.''

Clayt had no reason to believe that the old trail boss was exaggerating.

"Buck—how many hands are you short now?''

Tanner shrugged. "Ten now. Twice that fer a full crew. A couple left this week. Didn't stay. Musta fell out with Jake.''

Clayt pretended mild interest. "Harmer and I led in two horses from Tres Dedos tonight.''

"I know. I seen ya,'' Tanner replied. "I know them horses.''

"Oh?''

"Two fellas named Fowler and Stucey come down here about ten days ago and signed on. Jake found 'em in Vegas. Them and Jake went off on some kinda job a few nights back. Jake never did say what happened, but he come back alone. Nobody who's savvy will go askin' why. What he tells ya is all he wants ya to know.'' He chuckled. "If you want to stay healthy and eat reg'lar, son, that's all ya want to know.''

Clayt encouraged some aimless palaver, then got up to spread his bedroll on the straw-filled bunk and turned in. He was restless, troubled by the visions of the carnage on the dam and his father's dying injunction. Hatred burned in his throat. He could kill Jake Harmer with vicious pleasure, empty all six rounds into his rotten head. The more he thought of the pleasure it would give him, the more he knew he could not promise himself that one day he wouldn't, given the opportunity. "God knows," he whispered to himself, "I've got the reason!"

Chapter Five

Clayt rose before daylight and worked for an hour on a new corral. Breakfast was eaten in silence. When he returned to the job he grew aware of Jake Harmer's continued scrutiny. Just before noon dinner break, the foreman found some work to do nearby.

"Never did ask what side ya was on durin' the war," he said. "Mebbe ya was too young."

"Part of my family fought with Sibley," Clayt replied. "I didn't ask for it but they put me in the Quartermaster Corps."

Harmer snorted. "An eatin' outfit, not a fightin' outfit! By the time I was the age I figger you t'be now, I was ridin' with Quantrill. There wasn't no tougher, harder ridin', straighter shootin' outfit on two legs or four."

Clayt clamped his jaws to keep from responding. The double-bitted ax he was using to trim the corral poles burned in his hand. Harmer was about to launch into a detailed description of his infamous career when Buck Tanner called from across the yard.

"Hey, Jake! T.K. wants t'see ya, pronto!"

Clayt's lips were compressed in a thin, hard line as he watched the foreman hurry over to the house. He was about to resume his work when some movement in back of the house attracted his attention. A moment later a slender young girl with long dark hair emerged from behind a line of laundry. He watched as she disappeared carrying an empty hamper.

After the noon meal Buck came by the corral wearing an expression of abject disgust. Clayt glanced up, gave him a second look, and said, "What's the matter with you?"

Buck spat. "I gotta ride inta Vegas in the mornin'—an' have you got any idea what fur?"

" 'Fraid not."

"T.K.'s got me ridin' inta town to buy—ya ain't gonna believe this—dresses and things fur his housegirl!" He threw up his hands. "Kin you imagine what sorta talk I'm gonna hear when it gits around that I'm playin' nursemaid fur some poor kid he bought off'n the comancheros a couple a' weeks ago?" He thrust his head forward. "Kin ya, Clay?"

In spite of himself Clayt smiled. "Well, there's worse work." He glanced in the direction of the house. "You said, 'house girl.' I thought she must be Oakley's daughter."

"Daughter, hell! She ain't even no kin! He bought her off'n them comancheros fur a sack a' pronghorn jerky, some ammunition, and an old Smith and Wesson rimfire thirty-two."

He snorted in disgust. "Before he gits through with that poor chile, she's gonna wish she was anywhere but in that house. When an old guy like that starts fancyin' up a purty little thing, the plans he's got fur her ain't kindly mentioned in the Bible!"

He was still shaking his head as he left for the bunkhouse.

In midafternoon Jake Harmer came to the corral to saddle up. "I'm gonna look at some unbranded stock up on the edge of the mesa," he said. "When you finish them rails, Oakley wants to talk to ya."

"What's he want?"

"I don't ask him no questions like that." Smirking, he

added, "An' if you got any sense, you ain't gonna, neither!"

He aimed a warning finger. "An' I'll tell ya sumpthin' else—when I git back I'm gonna ask ya what he wanted, and yer gonna tell me—real truthful! Git it?"

Clayt looked him in the eye, smiled, and turned back to his work without answering.

Harmer started to jab a finger into his back and thought better of it. "Ya hear what I said, Clayton?"

Without turning, Clayt replied, "I heard you."

"Well now, that's real smart," the foreman said, "'cause mostly the ones who is deef is dumb, too, an' like snakebit steers an' horses with busted legs, we gen'lly gotta shoot 'em."

When he heard Harmer ride out, Clayt turned and watched him. Half aloud he said, "I swear to God, mister, Hell's going to seem like paradise before I get through with you!"

A half hour before sundown, Clayt put his tools in the shed, dusted off, and cleaned his hands and face in the trough. Blotting dry with a bandana, he headed across the barren, hard packed yard to the house.

When T.K. Oakley saw him coming he stepped out on the porch. Indicating a chair he said, "Sit down, Clayton. I want to talk to you."

When he had settled on the chair, the superintendent stood facing him. For a disconcerting time, he studied Clayt with eyes as impersonal as a desert reptile deciding the fate of a prey. Finally, his manner eased and he pulled over a chair.

"Jake tells me that so far you're a good hand—mind your business and do your work."

Clayt nodded. "I came here looking for work. I do what he gives me as best as I can."

"Seems so," Oakley agreed. "But would you call yourself an all-around hand?"

"I've worked cattle some. What I don't know I can learn.

Mostly, I did contract hunting for the Kansas Pacific.''

"Why'd you quit?''

"Railroads drove out the buff herds, and I got tired of killing.''

"Does the sight of blood bother you, Clayton?''

"Depends on whose blood it is,'' Clayt responded mildly.

Oakley was amused. "That can make a difference alright,'' he agreed. Crossing his long legs and settling his trouser over a pair of black snakeskin boots as he spoke he said, "Did Jake tell you we're going to take up a lot more range?''

"He said something about ten thousand head by next summer.''

"He told you right. That means I'm going to need men I can depend on. I've been watching you. Jake says you've had schooling. He says you're good with your head and your hands. If you pan out, Clayton, there'll be good work for you here, and a good payday. For special work, I pay bonus gold.''

He studied Clayt again, briefly. "It don't take a crack shot to hit a buffalo, even on the run. Just how good are you with a rifle?''

Clayt inclined his head. "Most generally I manage to hit what I'm aiming at.''

"How about a six-gun?''

"I can use one. I like my Winchester sixty-six better.''

Oakley was silent for a time but his gimlet eyes never left Clayt's face. "What about whiskey?''

"Don't drink it. A little beer now and then—if it's handy.''

"Whiskey and cows don't mix,'' Oakley said. It was a flat-out statement. "If I catch a hand drinking on a drive, he takes off right where he is with no back pay. He don't even ride back to get his belongings.'' He leaned forward. "The way you talk it seems that would suit you fine.''

"It would,'' Clayt replied.

Oakley uncrossed his legs.

"Alright, Clayton, you've got a place here. Jake gets a little snarly now and then, but if you mind your own business you'll have no trouble with him—or with me. Is that understood?"

Clayt's cryptic smile puzzled Oakley. "The safest bet you'll ever make, mister, is that I'll be finishing the business I set out to do."

Oakley's face hardened for an instant, then his manner eased. "Good!" He turned and glanced through the open parlor door. "How's the bunkhouse coffee?"

"Better than Tres Dedos."

The answer surprised him. He turned back and laughed, displaying a set of even white teeth, whiter still against his dark skin.

"That's probably still an insult but I'll let it pass." Turning back again he called, "Girl, fetch two coffees."

The man's cold, preemptory tone troubled Clayt.

They sat in silence until the young woman reappeared with the coffee. When she was about to set them on the table beside the superintendent he pointed. "Give the man one."

Clayt accepted the cup and said, "Thank you, Miss." The girl hesitated for an instant, as though the response had surprised her. When she returned to the parlor, Clayt was aware that Oakley was studying him intently. His eyes belied the smile.

"Guess you haven't seen a pretty lady for a while. Right?" There was no mistaking the implication behind his apparent amusement.

"I haven't been served by a lady in a good while," Clayt responded. "Guess I'm not used to it by now."

"That's just fine, Clayton," Oakley replied, "because depending on what kind of service you have in mind, don't count on getting any of it around here. Is that clear?"

Clayt's half smile was humorless. "That's plain enough."

The new man's responses made Oakley a bit uneasy but

he dismissed his vague annoyance. Ranch hands were not often as well-spoken as this one. If it turned out that he could be trusted, he'd be given work that Harmer's explosive temper made him unsuited to handle.

Settling back, Oakley lifted his cup. "Drink your coffee now, Clayton, and tell me what you know about the territory between here and Raton."

A half hour later, outside the bunkhouse, Clayt was stopped by Buck Tanner. The old trail boss looked pleased.

"Purty good, socializin' with Oakley already," he said. "Not even Jake gits an invite t'do that!" A quid shifted from one cheek to the other and his manner changed.

"Say, Clay, mind if I talk sorta private-like?"

"I suppose not. Walk with me to the corral shed." Tanner fell into step. When they entered the small building where the saddles were stored, Clayt left the door open. He stopped Buck when he started to close it. "Just leave it open unless you've got something to hide."

"I got nothing to hide, Clay," he replied in a defensive tone, "only I don't want nobody to hear."

Clayt braced himself on the edge of the harness-maker's stool. From the first he had pegged the old trail boss for a talker but so far he had not repeated anything that smacked of malicious gossip.

"What's on you mind, Buck?"

Tanner hesitated uncertainly, then flapped his hands.

"Well, fur openers, they's bin some big changes in the Gavilan since I come here back in 'fifty-eight. I hired on then as a flank rider and done good at it. But when the old trail boss didn't know how to turn a stampede in on itself, or how to give Injuns a steer to butcher fur not botherin' us, I got to be boss."

Anxious to avoid a long-winded yarn, Clayt cut in. "Good, Buck, but what do you want to talk private about?"

"About the changes goin' on since the new owners took over, a Chicago packin' man name of Tom Garner an' a real fine English gent name of Freebairn. They call him 'Sir Charles,' sort of a respectable way of usin' his first name, I guess...."

"What changes?"

"Well, when Oakley come up from Texas after Jake come first to git things set up—that's when the firin' started." He nodded toward the bunk house. "Only five of us left, an' the biscuit shooter—not countin' you."

"If they're going to build up herds, why would they let good hands go?"

"That's what I'm drivin' at. Jake sez Oakley may send fur some Texas hands that works his way. Prob'ly git 'em mostly from John Chism's spread at South Spring. If that-there's true, then they's about as rough a bunch of gun-slingers callin' themselves cowhands as ever's bin seen in these parts."

"How does any of that rub off on you or me?"

"Mebbe it don't, Clay," he admitted. "But I heard sump-thin' that might be interestin' to you." He explored the salt-and-pepper stubble on his cheek. "Oakley an' Harmer don't pay much mind to me when I'm working around and they's talkin'. I didn't snoop a' purpose, but I heard Oakley askin' Jake how good you was with a gun. He said he never seen ya wearin' one, only yer rifle in the boot."

"Usually I don't wear a rig," Clayt said. "I'm comfortable with the Winchester." He frowned. "What do you make of it?"

"I don't know fur sure, Clay. Oakley told Jake two things. He said to keep an eye on ya 'cause ya don't act or talk like a cowhand so he ain't sure of ya. An' he told him to fix it up so he could see ya shoot."

"What else?"

"Nuthin', 'cept one thing. Oakley and Harmer make no

bones about hirin' only men who are gun-handy. They gotta be dead shots. Jake told me that one time.'' He shifted uncomfortably.

"I figger the trouble is, nobody's seen ya wearing a rig."

"I own a forty-four. You could say I'm handy with it."

The old man looked relieved. "That's what Jake'll expect alright." He reached for Clayt's hand. "Son, I'm sure glad I spoke my piece! Me and the boys's is glad yer here, Clay. Yer way of talkin', an' all, makes ya differ'nt, but the crew likes that. It's only Oakley and Jake that's nervous."

Clayt gave Buck Tanner's upper arm a friendly squeeze. Easing off the stool, he said, "They'll find out about me in good time. I'm much obliged to you." In the doorway he paused. "And if Harmer gives me proper cause to shoot, I'll try real hard not to miss."

Clayt's quiet, matter-of-fact tone, left no room for doubt in the old trail boss's mind.

Chapter Six

Jake Harmer returned as the ember glow of sunset was fading. He put his horse in the corral and went directly to the main house. A few minutes later he appeared in the cookshack. Clayt was eating with Buck Tanner and the four remaining hands.

"I want to see you, Clayton, when you finish supper." He aimed his thumb in the direction of the corral. "There."

A few minutes later he found Harmer in the saddle shed. "You seen T.K.?"

"Yes."

"What did he talk about with ya?"

"He asked me some questions."

"What kinda questions?"

"The kind you asked me. I got the feeling he was checking to see if I told the same story twice."

Harmer snorted. "If you was as fast with a six-gun as y' are with yer mouth, Clayton, you'd be worth somethin' to this outfit."

Clayt's bleak smile was unsettling. "Well, I just may be."

"Be what?"

"Be worth something to this outfit."

Harmer smirked. "Mebbe. Anyways, saddle up at first

light and git the cook to make up some grub for both of us. Me and you's ridin' out right after chow.''

The next morning after breakfast, Clayt took his rifle and two packages of food and walked to the saddle shed. It was still dark inside. He lit the lantern and set the packages on a shelf. As he reached for the saddle slung over its rail, a start went through him. Hanging on the horn was his holster and cartridge belt with the forty-four in place.

"What in hell is going on here?'' he said aloud. Harmer answered from the deep shadows behind him.

"Ya hadn't oughta leave a fine rig like that hangin' around, Clayton. Somebody might take a fancy to it.''

Controlling himself, Clayt wheeled around. "I didn't leave it there! It was buckled in my saddle bag.''

Harmer laughed. "I know. That's where I found it.''

Anger flared in Clayt's eyes. "What call have you got to go through my gear?''

Still amused, the foreman moved into the dim light of the doorway. "I've bin wonderin' what that big bulge was. Thought it might be sumpthin' t'interest me if we was ridin' together. An' ya know sumpthin', it was.''

Suddenly he was threatening. "Ya lied to me, Clayton. Ya said ya didn't favor no six-shooters—only rifles.''

When Clayt moved a step closer, Harmer's hand dropped to his holster. "Before you go calling me a liar, mister, you better get the facts straight.'' Clayt's voice was cold and level. "I never said I didn't own a six-gun, and I never said I can't use one. I told you I favor my Winchester. There are seventeen shots in it and if a man knows how to handle a lever action, he can get them off straighter and as fast as any of your fancy gun slingers. Now you stop and think. Do you remember what you asked me?''

There was something about this new man's manner, the unafraid look in his eyes, that made Harmer control his desire to draw. Instead, he smirked.

"I did ask if ya could handle a six-gun," he admitted.

"And what did I say?"

Harmer shrugged. "Sumthin' like, 'depends.' "

"That's right. And what else did I say?"

"You favored your Winchester."

Clayt's manner eased a bit. "You got it right this time, Harmer. I favor my rifle. I can use it. And I can use a six-gun. When Oakley asked me which I favored, I told him the same thing."

Spreading his hands, Harmer said, "Now don't git no burr under yer tail, Clayton. I jes wanta know ever'thin 'bout a man 'afore I trust 'im."

"Well," Clayt said, "to ease your mind a little more, Harmer, I've never shot a man in the back and I've never shot helpless people."

Harmer tensed. "Jes' what does that figger t'mean?"

"You rode with Quantrill, you say. If you did, you've got to remember those hundred and fifty men, women, and children—or was that just a big lung-airing?"

"It wasn't no big talk," Harmer snapped defensively. "When there's a war on, innocent folks git in the way. I swear not a man of us—not even Bill Quantrill himself—set out to shoot women and children. Mebbe there's some that would, but ya'd never catch me doin' that!"

Clayton smiled at the man's choice of words. "Well Harmer, if anyone ever did catch you doing it, I'm sure the Good Lord would catch up with you, too. Life's like that!"

"I got no worry on that 'count, Clayton. Now, let's quit gabbin' and git goin.' "

For the first time since he had started working at Gavilan, Clayt buckled on his rig. Harmer watched him uneasily.

By midmorning the cloud cover had moved east and the sun burned down on the piñon-dotted mesa. Both men shed their vests and drank from canteens carried so their bodies would shade them.

The dry, erosion-fluted watercourse they were following became wider and shallower as they neared the river. Farther south the Pecos itself would widen some, but now it was a shallow, meandering stream divided by sand bars and shaded here and there by stands of gnarled cottonwoods that had survived the rush of spring floods.

When the horses smelled the water they quickened their paces and their heads tossed impatiently. Harmer cursed and jerked so hard the sharp tongue spade on the Spanish bit bloodied the animal's mouth. Clayt had a hard time containing his disgust.

Downstream several hundred yards, a small gather of longhorns were loafing at the water's edge. Harmer pointed to them.

"Them'll be Gavilan stock soon. We'll bring 'em in. If they ain't branded, they'll soon be!"

They rode down the shallow bank and reined up. Harmer dismounted and handed the reins to Clayt. "Hold him fur a minute. I wanta go lookin' fur something."

His needle-sharp Mexican rowels made pin prick tracks in the sandy mud as he jangled upstream a few yards. Clayt watched curiously as he stopped at the water's edge, then turned and walked to the nearby bank. A few more yards upstream he repeated the same move. Each time Clayt could see that he was examining a stone cairn piled around a limb that had been forced into the damp soil.

Harmer returned shortly and growled. "Those thievin' water hogs didn't waste no time fixin' their dam." He pointed to the rough monuments. "In normal times, them markers is almost at the water's edge. Now, they's high and dry and ten yards back!"

He remounted and let his horse join Clayt's who was nuzzling and slobbering the water. "That's a hell of a lot of water gone," he grumbled.

When they had approached the river, Clayt noticed the

recent high watermark. So far there had been no summer storms of any consequence in the Sangre de Cristo Mountains. The new line was formed by the sudden release of water from their dam. As he read the clear evidence again, Clayt's right hand found its way involuntarily to the stock of the Winchester resting against his leg. He wished again that he could gun Harmer down, go back and take out Oakley, and be done with it. The trouble was, if the Gavilan people wanted to drive his people off Red Creek there would soon be another Harmer to do their dirty work.

When he reined his horse's head up to keep him from over drinking he became aware that Harmer was standing watching him with an oddly twisted smile.

"Seen yer hand restin' on the Winchester, Clayton," he said. "Never did see ya shoot, did I?"

Inwardly startled, Clayt shook his head. "Guess not. Nothing worth wasting shells on."

Harmer's smile broadened and Clayt's stomach knotted as the foreman's Colt suddenly appeared. When the hammer clicked into cocked position, his scalp crawled.

Pointing with his weapon, Harmer said, "See that hunk of dead limb on the far bank? 'Bout man-sized, wouldn't ya say?"

An instant later the horses reared, a flock of birds exploded from a nearby cottonwood, and small animals scurried to burrows as Harmer fanned off three shots. The slugs all ploughed into the wood at extreme range. He ejected the casings and said, "Let's see you put three inta it from here, fast-firin' yer rifle."

The tension drained from Clayt as he unsheathed the Winchester. He checked the chamber, dismounted, and dropped the reins. As a target, the tree trunk Harmer chose was an easy shot for a rifle, even in unskilled hands. The foreman knew it. Smiling inwardly, Clayt sighted and put three shots into it with no special attempt at speed.

After the shower of rotting wood splinters settled, Harmer smirked. "Fair shootin', Clayton. Try sumthin' smaller." He pointed. "Git me one a' them groundhogs settin' away over yonder wonderin' what the hell's happenin'."

Clayt chose the most distant of three and without seeming to take special care with his aiming, fired. The small animal disappeared in a cloud of dust.

"Them groundhogs is fast," Harmer said. "Could be he seen the bullet comin', but ya skun up his dirt pile so I'm givin' ya the benefit of the doubt."

Indicating Clayt's forty-four, he said, "Y'seen me fan off three at what I was lookin' at. How about you returnin' the favor?"

Clayt glanced at him, then took his time slipping the Winchester into its boot. As he lowered his arm, he turned and drew in a single fluid movement. Three bullets slammed into three separate targets on the far side of the stream.

When the horses settled down, Harmer stood staring, slackmouthed. "Where'n hell did you learn to handle a gun like that?" he demanded.

Clayt smiled. "Where I learned is not important. The only important thing is that I *did* learn."

"Ya said ya was a buff hunter. I kin see ya learnin' to handle a rifle, even ridin' flat out. But you didn't learn to draw an' shoot like that practicin' on dead whiskey bottles."

Clayt reloaded and returned the forty-four.

"You can't kill anything that's already dead, can you?" Harmer's reaction to the question was a nervous smile.

There was very little talk on the ride back to the ranch as Jake Harmer undertook a quiet reassessment of this disconcerting stranger.

When they returned, Harmer went directly to the main house. A half hour later he appeared in the bunkhouse door.

"We got another job t'do, Clayton. When I told Oakley the water's not comin' through like it oughta, he said for us to ride in the mornin' and see how far along them sod-busters has got with fixin' their dam. This time he wants it blown to hell fur keeps.'' He jerked a thumb toward the main house. ''He wants me and you to figger out the best way t'do it.''

Cold anger and determination filled Clayt. If there's a God in heaven, he thought, He'll show me a way to stop these mad dogs—a way to finish them for good. After a long pause, he said, ''We can ride to the rim and look down without being seen, for all the good that will do. But is that man really fool enough to believe that they're going to leave their dam unprotected so we can go riding down there anytime we please?''

Harmer shot him a warning look. ''You watch that loose tongue of yours, Clayton. Oakley don't take kindly t'bein' called a fool!''

''And I don't care to be taken for the kind of fool who would walk into a sure trap,'' Clayt replied. His quiet voice and humorless smile once again angered Harmer but moved him to restraint.

''Nobody but them knows if they's a guard set, an' all we're gonna do now is scout the place. I done a lot of scoutin' fur Quantrill 'fore we rode in. 'Bloody Bill' Anderson and me scouted fur Red Legs before we hit Baxter Springs. We found 'em, took 'em out from behind, surprised over a hunn'erd Federals, an' kilt sixty-five of 'em. We was there and gone 'fore they knew which end of their guns did the shootin'. All T.K. wants now is fur us to look. The figgerin' kin be done later.''

Clayt's mind raced. Two things were clear. He would have to find a way to warn his people and figure out a way to trap Harmer in the act and hold him. There was no question that the foreman had acted under orders, but unless he could be forced into a confession that would stand up, it would simply be word against word and there was good reason to feel that the benefit of any doubt would go to the cattlemen. Oakley would have to be implicated, and perhaps the new owners as well.

"If there's a chance to do it and get out alive, when do you plan to try it?"

"It's dark moon in three nights," Harmer replied. "That's when Oakley wants it done. And," he added, "there's bonus gold."

Clayt thought for a moment. "I'll ride," he agreed, "but understand this—he can bust my pockets with gold, but if I think there's no way to get down there and out again, he can bribe somebody else to ride with you." Pointedly, he added, "Gold's no good in a dead man's pocket."

Clayt's afterthought made Harmer start. "What's that kinda talk mean?" He groped for words for a moment, then added, "My deal with Oakley don't include gittin' shot fur a fool, neither."

As Clayt walked away, Jake Harmer stood looking after him. Then he went to his own bunkhouse, lit the lamp, and poured himself a double shot of straight whiskey. From the first day, there had been something inexplicable about Clayton. He couldn't put a finger on it but he was certain now, especially after watching the man handle the Winchester and the heavy forty-four, that if he couldn't draw on him and surprise him, Clayton might be the one to walk away from that encounter, too. That T.K. Oakley was interested enough in the man to ask him to talk sociablelike, didn't bode well for him, either.

Oakley had education. He read books. He could talk to any man, high or low. Clayton could too. He'd given Clayton the job of figuring out the best way to wipe out the Red Creek people as though he himself couldn't do it alone.

Harmer took another four-finger shot of whiskey and smiled.

"Well, Mister Clayton, you ain' no cowhand and I know

it, an' that means on a drive a lotta things kin happen very nat'chly to a greenhorn who don't know the ways of the trail. Be a cryin' shame if I had to bring yer flea trap and things back to T.K. t'look fur yer next a' kin.''

They passed Tres Dedos at dawn. Riding at a lope, they turned west at the three large junipers that marked the little-used trail to the ford over the Pecos and on to the rim of Red Creek Canyon.

A few yards back from the head of the trail down to the settlement, they tethered their horses to some piñon trees and walked to the rim.

For a time they studied the scene below them. It was barely visible in the deep shadows. Lights were showing in the houses. Almost in answer to a prayer, as Clayt watched his own house, Nelda and Kate appeared in the doorway. Carrying a bucket, they went to the well. A minute or so later, Oss came out with his father. Clayt watched with a catch in his throat as they stopped to speak. Oss went on to the barn while Henry gathered an armload of stove wood.

"Look at 'em," Harmer growled, "goin' on like nuthin' happened.'' He pointed to the little burial ground almost directly below them on the near side of the creek. The moist earth of newly dug graves was clearly visible. Raw hatred boiled through Clayt again. He closed his eyes tightly to block out the horror of the vividly remembered scene.

"Jes look at 'em down there,'' Harmer sneered, "buryin' an' still patchin' like nuthin' happened. Well, purty quick you an' me's gonna be diggin' graves fur the rest of them stinkin' water thieves, just outta common decency.''

Standing close, Harmer felt Clayt's right arm jerk. "What in hell's th' matter with you, Clayton? You gettin' the nervous jumps already?''

Turning his back, Clayt stood in silence for a moment, trying to control a murderous rage. One push and he could send Harmer's ugly, squat body hurtling down into the canyon. That would be too good for him. If there was any justice at all, the vicious bastard would soon be doing the Mexican rope dance and he'd be there enjoying it down to the last twitch.

He glanced back at Harmer and returned to the horses. He was joined immediately. "What's the rush?"

"I've seen all I have to see. I've been down there."

Harmer bunched the reins and mounted. "D'ya think ya know what to do?"

Up beside him, Clayt turned his horse back to the trail.

"I know exactly what to do. Exactly!"

"Well, work fast! We only got a couple a' days."

Chapter Seven

Shortly after the midday meal, Clayt and Jake Harmer rode into the ranch headquarters. The cook rustled up bowls of tough beef chili and tortillas. Harmer wasted no time bolting the fiery concoction and stopped in the doorway.

"I'm gonna cut some fuse and time it," he said. "Oakley's got some of that new dynamite. I'm a black powder man. I don't cotton to that new stuff, but Oakley sez it's a hell of a lot stronger than powder." He stepped outside and turned back. "I want enough fuse to git clear. We gotta do this job right this time. T.K.'s real plain on that." He started to go and another thought stopped him again. "By the way, I told Oakley you was a purty good shot."

Clayt smiled as he watched him leave. He would have given a lot to have heard Harmer's response if Oakley had questioned him closely.

In the hot bunkhouse he found Buck Tanner stretched out on the top of his blankets. The old man propped himself up on an elbow.

"Seen ya ridin' out before sun up this mornin'," he said. "Looked like mebbe you and Jake was goin' some'ers."

Clayt smiled at Buck's usual attempt at fishing. They were harmless expeditions. In a dozen ways the old trail boss, who felt like a loner now, had let it be known that he wanted to be friends. There was no point in being evasive.

"We rode up to Red Creek."

Buck pushed himself upright and sat on the edge of the bunk. "Ya don't say! Jake's checkin' up on the dam, aint he?"

"That's right."

Buck wagged his head and chuckled. "He must be gittin lonesome in his old age—needin' company."

"I doubt it,"Clayt replied. "Oakley told him to take me along to look at the layout."

"Oh ho, there! That's right, Clay. You was down there. Ya borryed that horse." He frowned. "Wonder what them two is up to now? More trouble fur them settlers, I s'pose."

"That's right, Buck." Clayt decided to risk a leading question. "Tell me, do you believe they're hogging water?"

"Hell no! Onc't their pond's full, the same amount's gonna go spillin' over and run on downstream. If Oakley's worried, all he's gotta do is throw a couple 'a small dams across them fingers on the river durin' low water. He kin water a thousand head easy. Besides, them folks got rights, too."

"Forgetting the water," Clayt said, "do you think those people are in a position to hurt the Gavilan in any other way?"

Tanner was incredulous. "Why, you'd hafta be loco t'think that, Clay! I never did see no sense in harmin' them folks. I never met any of 'em, but livin' down there peaceful an' all, it stands t'reason they's the kind that wants to be left alone to mind their own Ps an' Qs."

"That's how I size them up too, Buck."

"Tell ya one thing, Clay, I'd trust 'em a whole lot further than Oakley and Harmer and their kind!"

"From what I know of them, I expect the settlers would trust you, too." Clayt replied.

It was obvious the old man was pleased. "How come ya say that?"

Clayt smiled. "Let's say I know people."

Buck Tanner's pleased look blossomed into a smile and he sawed at the base of his nose with a forefinger. "Well, 'cept fur the weather, an' cranky steers, people's all ya ach'ally gotta t'know real good t' git along in this world."

Clayt sat down beside him, tugged gently at the toes of his heavy gray wool socks. His sister Fern had knitted them for him and it looked like they'd soon need a little darning. After her death he had considered tucking them away as a keepsake but practical necessity ruled that out for now.

In the silence that followed, Clayt mulled over the possibilities he had considered on the ride back to the Gavilan. If no other chance remained to warn his people, then he would break his pledge. He knew there was no way he could leave both Oakley and Harmer alive to murder and destroy a second time.

If he was forced to kill both men, they would still have to go to the law, but it would be useless one-sided testimony unless somebody from the Gavilan who knew what was going on could be induced to speak up as a witness.

"Buck," he said, "I've got another question for you."

"Fair 'nuff, Clay. Spill it."

"Do you really know what went on down at the Red Creek settlement, beyond the blowing of their dam?"

Tanner thought a moment then shook his head. "Nope."

"You didn't know that Harmer and his two gunslingers not only blew up the dam but murdered fourteen of the settlers in cold blood?"

The old trail boss looked as though he hadn't heard correctly. His face screwed up and he leaned closer. "Fourteen—killed?"

"Fourteen men, women, and children, Buck, shot dead in the middle of the night when they came running out to see what had happened. Fourteen dead, Buck—a dozen others wounded. Some will die.''

Tanner closed his eyes and ran a horny hand over his face. "Lord A'Mighty, Clay," he said in a hoarse whisper, "that-there's a massacree!" Opening his eyes he added, "Y'mean t'tell me that Harmer and them two done a thing like that—almost like Lawrenceville all over?"

"That's right."

"But how d'ya know that? Fur sure, I mean?"

"You take my sworn word, Buck. Now here's another question. Why do you think those two men Harmer hired went out with him and didn't come back—only their horses?"

"Yeah, Clay—I know." The old man's voice was still choked with disbelief. "I thought on that, but I sure as hell wasn't gonna ask Jake Harmer no questions." He drew in a deep breath and leaned back. "I 'spect ya know why Stucey an' Fowler—them's the names they give—didn't come back?"

"They didn't come back, Buck, because Harmer shot them dead in the saddle, probably to keep their mouths shut after they helped him. He took their horses and their guns and stripped their pockets. I know he gave them each twenty dollars in gold against a promised forty dollars a month. He rode into Vegas a day or so later and used the money he had paid them and bought himself that fancy saddle and bridle.''

Unable to accept such depravity, even in a frontier territory where he knew from bitter personal experience that violence was not uncommon, the old trail boss wagged his head as though trying to reject the obvious truth.

"I repeat, Buck, it's the truth. The God's honest, hard-to-swallow truth," Clayt said gently. "I hope you believe that.''

Buck looked up and the sudden hopelessness he felt could be clearly read in his eyes. "I b'lieve ya, Clay, even though in the beginnin' ya played close to the vest. I b'lieve ya, son. I sure do.''

"You believe me enough to keep a promise if I ask you to?''

"They ain't no question, son.''

Clayt rested a hand on his shoulder and shook it affectionately. "Tell me something, Buck, why do you call me 'son'?''

Buck took so long to answer that Clayt came close to regretting the question.

"Well,'' he said. "onc't, a long time ago, back home—'twas eighteen-an'-thirty-three—I had me a fine wife an' she soon give me a fine boy. We decided t' move west to Missoura t'make a better life. I worked the sun up and down and got me a stout wagon and a sound team. In the spring of 'thirty-eight we set out.''

"By fall we had got as fur as a little place called Haun's Mill. Already it was bitter cold, so we decided to winter there near some Mormon folks who'd settled.

"They was fine, hard workin' people an' they liked the way I worked. So one day they come over and asked me an' the wife t' join 'em. We thought serious about it. Then one mornin' before they knew what struck 'em, a mob come ridin' in and kilt off half of 'em—mostly men and boys. My little son was playin' with some a' theirs''—his voice came near breaking—"an' they kilt him too.''

Suddenly, all of the repressed pain and anger flooded through Clayt and he wondered how long it would be before he could forget. Buck Tanner was still hurting after thirty years.

Forcing himself to continue, the old trail boss said, "I didn't have no idea at the time that th' Mormon people was run outa ever' place they settled. Seems the governor of Missoura hated 'em, too—so much he give an order to kill 'em off and drive 'em out wherever they was found.''

"My little wife didn't last long after that." He folded his arms and pressed them hard against his middle. "My son, Tom, woulda bin some older'n ya, Clay," he said in a barely audible voice, "an' I'll tell ya the truth, I'da bin mighty happy if he'da growed up bein' some like ya...."

The pair lapsed into a thoughtful silence, then Clayt stirred and got up.

"You want to know why I know it's the truth. Right?"

"I said I b'lieve ya, Clay. I do."

"Well, friend, so there won't be even the smallest bit of doubt, I was down in Red Canyon when it happened."

Buck sat bolt upright. "Am I hearin' right? You was there?"

"I was there. They killed my father and my sister...and twelve others."

The old man jumped up. "My Gawd A'mighty, Clay, you gotta be one of 'em!"

"I am, Buck. I rode in here pretending to look for work after I found out in Las Vegas that Harmer hired on these two killers there. Nobody knew them in Vegas. They were strangers. My friend and I found their stripped bodies at the top of our trail."

Clayt paused to let the words sink in. "I came here to get proof. I've got it now, but I need someone to help me."

Buck Tanner reached out and took Clayt's hand in both of his.

"You got 'im, son! You got 'im! I swear on my baby boy's grave, you got 'im!"

For the first time since Harmer had arrived at the Gavilan Buck Tanner felt he had a reason for being. "Ya knnow sumpthin' Clay, even though I knowed that Jake Harmer learned killin' with Quantrill, I never really figgered him fur cold-blooded murder. I figgered it was sumpthin' ya had t'do durin' a war, an' then ya got a bellyful and was glad t'quit."

"That's how my people felt, Buck. They had enough

fighting the Union troops.'' The old man aimed a finger at him.

"But Harmer ain't cut like that! So now he wants t'go down there and finish the job, an' that black-eyed diamondback 'spects ya to help him!'' He dry-spat in disgust.

"I'm going to help alright—help both of those murdering monsters stick their necks right into a noose,'' Clayt replied, "and that's why I'm going to need some help from you.''

"Jes' tell me what, son.''

"My people will go to the law as soon as I can trap Harmer in the act and we can force a confession out of him—one that will trap Oakley and maybe the new owners, too.''

Tanner cocked his head and frowned. "Can't say I know about Tom Garner and this Sir Charles fella. I seen 'em, of course, but I didn't drink no tea with 'em.''

Clayt smiled. "You said people were all you really have to know in this life. Didn't you size them up at all?''

"They's diff'rint, one from t'other, fur sure, but they's the same in their talk about what they want fur the ranch. When they first come, an' I drove 'em down from Vegas, they talked business. I got the notion that they want a top notch, money-makin' spread, but they was talkin' more about the quality of the stock than almost anything else. They was talkin' real serious about bringin' over from Europe some shorthorn breedin' stock that wasn't so tall and stringy-meated as longhorns. In the three hours I drove 'em, I didn't hear nuthin' that made me think they would kill t'git their way.'' He paused thoughtfully. "I gathered they was happy to git Oakley 'cause of his rep'tation as a stockman. I didn't hear 'em mention a word 'bout Harmer.''

'Well, Buck, if I can trap Harmer and get him to talk— and he will, as God is my witness—he'll spread the blame. We'll find out about the others later. In the meantime, when and if we get Harmer to the law, we're going to need proof that somebody who works for Oakley and Harmer knew about their plans to drive out my people. That means testifying in court."

Clayt saw a fleeting shadow of uneasiness in Tanner's eyes.

"That's what I want you to promise me you'll do."

"Well now, Clay," the old man temporized, "ya know I didn't ach'ally see no killin'...."

"I know that, Buck. But you did hear them planning to drive out the settlers by blowing up their dam."

"Yes, sir, I did!"

"And you are willing to tell the court that much—only the truth—nothing else?"

Buck Tanner thrust out his hand. "That's eg-zac'ly what I'll do, son. Eg-zac'ly!"

Chapter Eight

Clayt spent the rest of the day finishing some work on the corral gate. After supper he discouraged Buck from more reminiscing. He needed time to think. The odds against getting down in the canyon to warn his people were far worse than he had allowed himself to believe. More than that, the chances of working out an effective trap were less than marginal. He wondered at the providence that had led his father and Henry Deyer to the canyon in the first place.

"You can't make things un-happen," his mother had observed once when an earlier bit of ill fortune had beset them. "All you can do is dig in and start over."

But there would be no new beginning unless there was a certain and lawful end to Oakley and to Harmer and to anyone else who might have influenced their attempt to run off his people. As impatient as he was, Clayt knew that his father's counsel had been right. Perhaps another sort of providence had led him to share a bunk house with old Buck Tanner.

If Buck did speak up in court against the new Gavilan plan, there would be no place for him here under any circumstances. He had given that some thought too. But Buck would have a place with his people if he wanted one. He'd see to that.

Moseying to the corral, Clayt fondled the buckskin mare's velvety nose. She gave him a thank-you nuzzle as he climbed up to perch on the top rail.

He sat there going over possible alternatives until it was full dark. Deeply engrossed in decisions that could spell life and death for himself and the others, he did not see a small figure come out of the darkness on the far side of the corral, pause for a moment, then scurry silently to the deep shadow of the hay barn.

Clayt yawned, eased to the ground, and took a step or two toward the bunk house. Except for the crystal glitter of the stars, the night was velvety black. The evening breeze was cool now but strong enough to rustle the big leaves on the sycamores by the bunk house. In the distance, the main house was dark except for the pale orange glow of a lamp in a side window.

He could see the open door of the bunkhouse. No smokey lamp glow was visible. He hoped he would hear Buck's peculiar tattered snoring. The four remaining hands would probably be sleeping too. For several days, Harmer had set them to riding some miles up and down the river in search of stray longhorns who would be rounded up and branded, or whose brands would be changed, as Oakley began to build up his first herd.

Harmer had told him that T.K. Oakley lived by himself for the time being, that his wife in El Paso would join him when she was ready.

"I know the lady," Harmer had said, "an' I'll gar'ntee it aint no love match between them two. She likes her fancy friends an' her fancy clothes, an' ya oughta see her struttin' 'em around!"

The light was probably in the room where Oakley's housegirl stayed. From the amount of work she had to do, she'd be up late, he thought.

Clayt turned when he heard the little buckskin move away to the far side of the corral and whinney softly. He wondered about it. Sometimes a stray burro or even a hungry pronghorn would wander over looking for fallen hay. Curious, he walked around the railings. As he reached the far side of the enclosure, he stopped short and listened. Something had let out a plaintive cry. Possibly it was a ranch cat.

A moment later he heard the sound again and this time it was clearly made by a human—a frightened, childish sob. The mare was listening with her ears cocked and her head turned to the left. Speaking softly to her, Clayt moved cautiously through the deep shadows. The sobbing sound had stopped. He moved a few more steps and suddenly, not six feet from him, a small female figure leaped up with a panicky cry and fled toward the barn.

In a half dozen long strides, Clayt caught her by the arm. He stifled the beginning of a scream with his hand. "Be quiet!" he ordered in a hoarse whisper. "I'm not going to hurt you. You'll be alright."

The girl twisted her face free and gasped, "Please don't take me back—don't let him get me. Oh, God, please..."

Clayt muffled her face against his shirt. "You're alright, Miss! Nobody's going to hurt you." He pressed her head closer and slipped an arm around her tiny waist to stop the trembling. Her skin was damp with perspiration and he could feel that her dress was torn at the top of the skirt.

"You're Oakley's housegirl," he whispered. "What happened?"

A violent shudder shook her but she did not answer.

"Did he hurt you?"

The girl nodded and turned to press her cheek against his chest. Cradling her head, Clayt said, "You're all right now, Miss. I'm not going to let anybody hurt you. Was it Oakley who frightened you?"

Her head moved under his hand. "He wanted to use me..." She began to shake again, violently, and pressed her face closer.

The girl's plight awakened an old protectiveness in Clayt, one that he had not felt since his young sister, Nelda, had come running to him to be saved from a dozen imaginary dangers.

"Please," the girl pleaded, "I can't go back. It was all right at first"—she broke off and shuddered—"but tonight he..." She broke off again and lapsed into dry sobs.

All at once it seemed to Clayt that providence was still conspiring to complicate his life. He knew that if he turned the girl over to Oakley she would fare little better than if she had remained with the comancheros. If he allowed her to flee wearing only a torn dress and kaibab moccasins, Clayt was certain she would not last the night on the mesa. If by some chance she did, Oakley would set a crew to tracking and they'd find her—or what was left of her.

In the midst of his quandry he heard a door slam at the main house. Three hundred yards away Oakley appeared carrying a lantern. Clayt held his breath for a few seconds, then lifted the girl's chin and pressed his fingers against her lips. "Be quiet now," he warned. "Don't make a sound!" He glanced back then picked her up like a child and hurried to the barn.

Inside, he pointed to the hay loft. "Climb up there real quick! Cover your face with your skirt and bury yourself in the hay. He's coming. He'll likely look for you in here. Don't move. Don't make a sound," he repeated. "I'll be back in a little while. Can you ride?"

"Yes...."

"Good! If Oakley gives up looking there'll be a mare with a bridle and a surcingle waiting. I'll get you on it and tell you where you can go to be safe. Do you understand?"

"Yes...yes," she whispered, "...Oh, God...thank you!"

"If this works," Clayt whispered, "thank God, not me!" He boosted her up. "Now get in there and cover up. When I get back I'll call out, 'Everything's ready!' Don't you make a peep for any other voice."

Clayt waited until he heard the scrambling stop, then he hurried to the barn door. T.K. Oakley, in trousers and an unbuttoned undershirt, was holding the lantern high to peer inside the cookhouse. Clayt ran to the back door of the barn, skirted the corral by a wide margin, cut to the rear of the bunkhouse, and ducked into the privy. He lit the candle there and prepared to wait. If Oakley looked in the bunkhouse and found his bed empty, he would avoid any questions by returning in full view.

Clayt watched from the outhouse door. When he saw Oakley disappear into the barn he held his breath. After an anxious several minutes, the man reappeared and carried the lantern around the corral, then cut across the yard to his house.

Clayt waited until he saw him go inside. The chances were that the superintendent was going to put on more clothes and search a wider area. When he was reasonably certain he could get away with it, he ran to the saddle shed, took down a spare bridle and gathered up a length of halter rope.

When the mare heard him approach, she came to the gate. He let himself in, gentle-talking her as he moved, and slipped the bit into her mouth. Next he tied a figure eight double loop for a handhold and threw the improvised surcingle over her back. Then, moving carefully, he cinched the ends under her belly, led her to the gate, and fastened the reins to the rail.

Satisfied, he hurried around the corral to the barn and stepped up on the edge of the manger.

"Everything's ready," he called in a loud whisper. When there was no answer he pulled himself up into the loft and called again.

Just beyond him there was a rustling in the hay and the girl appeared. He slipped a hand under her arm.

"Hurry up now. There's a good mare waiting for you. I'll get you on her. Ride easy until you're clear of the main ranch gate, then give her her head. Ride straight up the Vegas road to Tres Dedos. The place is just an adobe on the right and a couple of sheds and a corral. Have you got that?"

"Yes, I think so...."

"About a mile beyond, a trail takes off on the left for the river. It's just a few yards past a stand of three big junipers. It's not well marked but the mare will find it. Stay on that trail. Cross the river—it's shallow now—and give the mare her head—follow the trail up the bank and stay on it until you get to the rim of Red Canyon. Go down that trail. Again, let her have her head. There may be guards. If you are stopped, tell them that Clayton sent you. Remember that name—Clayton—tell them Clayton Adams wants you to go to his mother's house and wait there. I promise you'll be welcome."

He went over the directions again, then lifted her down from the loft. At the corral, after a precautionary look around, he boosted her on the mare and whispered, "With good luck you'll make it about sun up."

Clayt slapped the mare gently on the rump and started it off at an easy trot. When the girl disappeared in the darkness, he returned to the bunk house, slipped off his boots, and stretched out on the straw mattress. For the next few minutes he came as close as he ever had to praying.

Nineteen-year-old Kate Williams rode the mare with the ease of one who had been raised to ride since childhood.

She let the mare find its own quickened pace. In two hours she reached Tres Dedos. No light was showing but she held her breath when one of the horses in the corral whinnyed softly. In a few more minutes she was out of sight.

She thought of the man who had come to help her. He said his name was Clayton. In the darkness she couldn't be sure, but he must have been the one to whom she had served coffee. The possibility worried her. What if he really was one of Oakley's trusted hands? In the next instant she dismissed the notion. If so, why had he risked his neck to save her?

Several minutes at an easy lope brought her to a stand of piñon. Slowing, she peered ahead and breathed a sigh of relief when the silhouettes of three large junipers could be made out against the starlit sky. In less than a minute the mare insisted on turning to the left. She slacked the reins and found herself following just a trace of a trail. Clayton had said that she should reach the trail leading down into Red Canyon around sun up. She glanced at the sky. There was no hint of the new day so she resigned herself to another hour of riding to reach the river.

She heard the water running over a gravel bar before she could see it. She would have expected the mare to have sensed water earlier but she had not been hard ridden.

The air was cool and fresh at the water's edge. She let the mare drink and enjoy the feel of the current against her fetlocks, then urged her up the far bank. The trail was easier to follow now.

Sensing an end to the journey, the mare quickened her pace. In less than a half hour Kate found herself at the head of the Red Creek Canyon trail.

A minute or two of exploring and the trail down to the settlement could be clearly read. Another well-defined trail led off to the northeast toward Las Vegas. She sat looking down for a minute. Lights were showing in two houses and a carried lantern bobbed along the edge of a pond off to her right.

Kate started when the mare suddenly whinneyed and tossed her head.

"What is it, girl?" she said. The words were hardly out when she heard the muffled thud of hooves below her. There was scarcely time to turn the mare when a horse being spurred to a labored uphill gallop burst into view not ten feet away.

Both riders uttered startled exclamations. Oss jerked a rifle free and chambered a shell. When he realized he had heard a female voice he lowered the rifle and rode closer.

"Who are you?" he demanded. "What are you doing here?"

"I'm looking for the Adams house," Kate managed in a small voice pinched with fright. "A man named Clayton at the Gavilan Ranch told me to come here and find his mother and sister."

"Clayton? Is Clayt alright?" he blurted.

"I think so—I hope so," she replied. "He risked his life to get me here." She broke off uncertainly. "I'm Kate Williams."

Returning the rifle to its boot, Oss said, "I'm Oscar Deyer—they call me 'Oss.' I'm Clayt's best friend. I'm riding down to Gavilan now—to see if he needs help."

"He might," Kate replied. "The comancheros sold me to a man named Oakley. He's the superintendent. I was to be his housegirl, but I couldn't do it. I ran away. Clayton found me hiding and helped me. If they find out about it, he'll be in bad trouble."

Oss reached into his saddle bag and removed a block of matches. He struck two and held them high. The face he saw would be pretty, but now he was looking into hollow, fear-filled eyes. In the half light he more felt than saw the fatigue-drawn lines, unmistakable signs of an ordeal that matched his own.

"If Clayt sent you, Miss, you are surely welcome here." Glancing at the sky he saw that sunrise was still minutes away. He had stood the last watch near the top of the trail in order to get an early start. John Bates would still be on guard at the bottom. Briefly, he debated the wisdom of letting the girl ride down the trail by herself, then decided against it.

"Come on," he said. "I'll take you down. Can you manage without a saddle? It's more than just steep."

"I'll be alright," Kate replied. She patted the mare's neck. "She has good sense."

It took a half hour to negotiate the treacherous trail, still dark in the depths of the canyon. Near the bottom Oss called out and John Bates emerged from a clump of cover.

"Mary's got unexpected company, John," he said. "This is Kate Williams. She's been through a lot. She'll be with us for a while. Clayt sent her."

The former Confederate corporal touched his finger to the brim of his hat in an implied salute and said, "Glad to have you here, Miss."

On the slow ride down Oss had asked Kate discreet questions. Her answers had been brief. Her family had been killed by Comanche raiders who destroyed their modest ranch in the Texas Panhandle. She and her brothers had been kidnapped and later, she was sold to the Comancheros who eventually sold her to T.K. Oakley. She avoided the embarrassing reason for her desperate flight. She preferred to say only that the man had been cruel.

As Bates returned to his post Oss called back, "I'm riding out again in just a little. Kate doesn't think anyone followed her but keep a sharp eye out just the same."

Minutes later Mary Adams and Nelda were alarmed at the sound of horses crossing the dam. When they stopped in front of the house Nelda came out. When she saw Oss, panic seized her. "What are you doing here? Is something wrong?" Mary came out immediately. Almost afraid to ask, she echoed the question.

"Everything's alright," he assured them. Turning, he pointed to Kate. "This is Kate Williams. She was working at the Gavilan. Some bad things happened to her. She had to get away. Clayt risked his neck to help her escape. He wants her to stay with you two until he gets back."

The older woman pushed past her daughter and moved to the buckskin mare. "Of course, Kate! Of course! But tell me, is Clayt alright?"

"Yes, ma'am, I believe so...I hope so...."

"My God, so do we," Nelda breathed as she rested her hand against Oss' stirrup. "We think it's a foolish thing he's doing. He's frightened us half to death!"

Ignoring Nelda, Mary motioned to the girl.

"Get off the mare, Kate. Come on in. You must be wrung out, child!"

Kate dropped the reins and slipped off easily. In the dim light from the doorway what Mary Adams' perceptive eyes saw made her throat catch. Turning to the door, she said, "Come in, child. You'll be safe here."

Oss leaned over and gathered the mare's reins. "I'll take her to the barn and keep her out of sight, just in case."

Nelda took the reins from Oss. "I'll lead her for you. I want to talk."

When she returned some minutes later, she found her mother seated next to Kate Williams at the long, polished plank table. At the end of her endurance, the girl had slumped over her thin bare arms.

Indicating a bowl of porridge, Mary said, "Force yourself

to eat a little, Kate. It will stick to your ribs. We just can't wait to hear about Clayt. And tell us all you care to about your trouble, dear. It's hard sometimes to talk about tearful things. We know!''

When the girl did not answer, the older woman lowered her head to conceal the threat of fresh tears. ''My God,'' she half whispered, ''we know about those murderers at Gavilan. They killed my husband and my older daughter and a dozen others including Oss' young brother...." She broke off, unable to continue for a moment. ''My son Clayton hired on there to try to get the proof we'll need to go to the law. The men at Gavilan don't know any of us, but it doesn't make any difference. I can hardly sleep nights from worrying that something will happen to him.''

Nelda brought a pot of fresh coffee and sat down beside her mother. ''I worry too, Kate. Oss and I are planning to get married, but without Clayt to take my father's place as head of this settlement, I don't know how we'd get on. We all, young and old alike, look to him. We look to Oss's father too, but he's not young anymore. After Oss's mother died three years ago, and then his young brother Ned died from the wound he got when they tried to drive us out, he's not the same. He's turned into himself.'' She slipped an arm around her mother's shoulder. ''Clayt's always been the strong one, ever since we were kids down in Texas.''

On the verge of collapse, Kate listened and understood. It would take such a man, she thought, to run the risk Clayton had taken to get her safely out of Oakley's grasp. She closed her eyes and let herself feel again the vast relief and security that she had known for scant minutes when he had carried her to the barn. Cradled in Clayt's arms, his strong fingers pressing through her hair to hold her face against his shoulder, she relived for a fleeting moment now, those times a dozen years earlier when her father had come to her rescue after some childish mishap. For her, tears also threatened again as she tried to blank out, but could not, the nightmarish tragedy of the Comanche raid and the sight of her father's using his rifle as a club when the ammunition was spent, going down, at last, with a huge long-bladed Bowie knife plunged deep into his back. She could not recall her own screams, but the echoes of her small brothers' terrified outcries as they were taken away would haunt her for the rest of her life. She shuddered and Mary pulled her close to comfort her. In a gentle voice, she said, "I know, Kate, I know, but please believe that you are safe and welcome here now. Whatever happened down there is over now. You'll be with us, dear child. You'll not be alone again —ever."

Unable to control herself, Kate gave in to an irrepressible sob, then collapsed with her head on the table and surrendered to a flood of long-denied tears.

In the Gavilan ranch house, filled with a rage reborn of frustration, T.K. Oakley's obsidian eyes glittered as he stretched out bootless and down to his underwear on the rumpled bed where he had tried to take her, his first in-house woman, the first one since he left behind El Paso and his wife of seven years, the attractive, arrogant Roberta Preston, the only daughter of Hobwell Preston.

A New Yorker, "Hobby" Preston had gone to Alabama as a commissioner in the Federal Freedmen's Bureau. Within months, seeing the possibility to fatten himself at the Reconstruction pork barrel, he had become a ruthless carpet-bagger by allying himself with like-minded Southern scalawags.

In 1869 he left Alabama accompanied by two Northern deserters who acted as his well-paid bodyguards. In his wagon were six capacious carpetbags and four heavy leather Spanish trunks filled with gold, silverware and plate, and fine jewelry swindled from destitute plantation owners' widows for two pennies on the dollar.

Seated beside the bodyguard handling the wagon team, was eighteen-year-old, shabbily dressed Roberta playing the convincing role of the tender young daughter coming West to Texas to forget the horrors of war.

T.K. Oakley groaned inwardly as he stared at the ceiling shadows cast by the guttering oil lamp. For six years he had not been able to rid his mind of that first meeting with Roberta, by then one of the best-dressed and most glamorous young ladies in El Paso's small but blossoming society. It had not bothered him—on the contrary he was pleased— that despite their twenty-year age difference, she seemed to favor him far more than any of the younger, overeager swains.

They were engaged in three months and married in six. Mutual friends said confidently that each had married the "catch of the year." He tossed restlessly as he remembered their wedding night and the honeymoon days and nights that had followed. Again, he damned her to hell and back, and damned himself too, for being so slow to understand that she had married him to prove that she could trap an eligible older bachelor who could give her everything she wanted, that all of the implied promises in her alluring coquetry had been the hollowest of pretenses.

Within six more months, puzzlement had turned to disbelief and then to loathing. When he had spoken to her father, in search of an answer, the older man had patted his arm and said, "Well now, T.K., you just keep on taking care of her and making allowances. After all, you're the first man she's ever had. Life's not been a bed of roses for the child since my wife died. You keep her in the pretty things she loves so much and she'll come around. Women always do.''

T.K. remembered now that by the end of the first year, he was beyond caring. The night after their first-anniversary dinner, in a fury of frustration, he had gone to one of the public houses along the river road, and later had crossed the Rio Grande bridge into Mexico and visited one of *las casas publicas*. No pretense there! The welcome was genuine. Pesos were exchanged for favors, and the bargain was honest.

He laughed bitterly and thought of the girl he had bought from the comancheros. There was no pretense in her either! Her terror was as real as his own need for her.

He shook his head violently and swung his legs off the bed. For a moment he sat undecided, then he got up and crossed the hall to the girl's room. One of the two new gingham dresses he'd sent Buck Tanner to buy for her hung on a peg. Beneath her couch was an indian basket holding her pitifully few personal belongings. Beside the basket was a pair of worn Mexican *huaraches*, the primitive sandals she wore around the house.

For a time he stood visualizing the girl as she must look when she was getting ready to sleep, thin and worn from her captivity. Rope burns were still visible on her ankles and wrists where the comancheros had trussed her at night. There were no garrisoned forts nearby, otherwise he knew she would have been forced into prostitution. She was not sick or she would not have survived those weeks on the trail with that half-breed gang. Thin she was, he thought, but with the promise of good breasts and provocative hips. A few more months of decent food and safe shelter, and the promise would be fulfilled.

In his room again he removed his long cotton underwear and black socks, stretched out, and pulled a light cotton

army blanket over his lower body. She was out there somewhere, hiding. Let her go through a night on the mesa. She'd
be more than willing to come back. He'd handle her fear
of him by threatening to turn her out. She'd get over it once
she understood that the security he would give her would
be worth the price that one day she would be willing to
pay. He would ask no more of her than that—that and total
obedience.

Chapter Nine

At sun up, when Clayt left the bunkhouse for the cook shack, he saw T.K. Oakley riding his big gelding up the Las Vegas road. Clayt watched him, studying the dusty tracks. Just before he reached the main gate with its crudely painted hawk nailed to the overhead cross piece, he pulled up, hesitated for a moment, then decided to turn right through the mesquite and scrub oak. To the east a few yards, a shallow barranca angled across the mesa, passed south of the buildings, then swung right and petered out in a sandy splay as it reached the Pecos. It was deep enough for cattle to hide in, and a girl could easily conceal herself there, too.

When Oakley eased the horse down the bank and disappeared, Clayt hurried to the cook shack. Harmer looked up from a bowl of yellow cornmeal mush, "What kept ya?"

Clayt ignored the question, got his food and coffee, and settled on the bench a few feet away.

"I said, 'What kept ya?' " Harmer repeated.

"Nothing," Clayt replied. "I'll be finished when you are."

The retort made the other four hands exchange nervous glances. Any friction between the new man and the foreman now had possible dangerous consequences since both men were wearing their six-guns.

Ignoring the rebuff, Harmer poured another coffee and

stood up. Calling down the long table to the men, he said, "There's a dozen mavericks northeast of the gate about a mile. They're loafin' in the scrub. Run 'em in and brand 'em, then haze 'em down toward the river with them others."

He put down his cup and moved toward the door.

"Let's git goin', Clayton."

Again there was no answer as Clayt pulled his legs free of the bench and followed Harmer out of the cook shack.

As they moved toward the corral, the foreman chuckled. "You see Oakley ridin' out early, lookin'?"

"I did," Clayt replied.

"T.K. sure as hell aint happy. Seems like his purty little filly jumped the fence last night."

Clayt shrugged. "Guess that's his problem."

"And the girl's," Harmer said smirking, "an' mebbe yourn too."

Clayt stopped. "What do you mean 'mine too'?"

"Well, the girl stole the buckskin mare you like."

"Guess she knows horses," Clay replied.

"She took a bridle, too, an' rode off bareback sometime in the night." He eyed Clayt suggestively. "If ya had yur eye on her, it's a shame t'lose a purty lil' filly, ain't it?"

"I have my eye on nothing that isn't strictly my business," Clayt replied flatly.

"Sure. Sure." Harmer slapped his leg and hitched at his denims. "He's either gonna take her t' bed and break her in good, or kill 'er." The thought made him guffaw. "I sure wisht he'd give me the job. I'd fatten her up, and sure as hell, when I was done teachin' her, she'd be a willin' woman!"

There could be no end to the loathing Clayt felt for Jake Harmer. When he had carried the girl from the corral to the barn, and later when he had held her to reassure her, the feel of her body, a woman's body for all of its slenderness, had reawakened half-denied longings that had become a part of a troublesome preoccupation that robbed him of sleep. His mother had often said that Hazel Coates was as beautiful and fragile as a finely painted figurine of English porcelain. From time to time he wondered—still did occasionally—whether Hazel might have survived the virulent tick fever if she had not been so finely made and fragile. Some of the sturdier ones had. Oakley's housegirl, as he called her, was not one such.

At the corral, Harmer pointed to the shed. "I'm gonna fuss with some fuse. Finish up them gate braces. After supper we can time some burnin'. The biscuit shooter's saved me some little bakin' soda cans that'll make real good hand bombs—just in case we need 'em."

A step or two in the lead, Harmer chuckled and shook his head. "Yes sir," he said to himself, "I'd sure learn that skinny little kid."

The vision of the stinking, foul-hearted foreman rutting over the girl sickened Clayt. He would spare a rabid coyote before he'd spare Harmer if his father's pledge had not stayed him.

Clayt followed him into the shed. He gathered his tools and left to finish his work on the corral. Engrossed, he did not look up until two proud cut stallions in the *caballada* started to whinny. When the whinnying became more persistent, he did look up and a shock ran through him. Oss was riding into the ranch at a fast walk.

Unable to believe his eyes, Clayt dropped the tools, shot an apprehensive glance toward the open shed door, and ran down the road to intercept him.

Signaling for silence, he grabbed Oss' mount by the bridle and pulled it up short. "Keep your mouth shut!" he called in a hoarse whisper. "I'm alright." He jerked his head toward the corral. "The man we want is in that shed. Tell Henry I'm coming down tonight—late. I'll leave my horse up top.

Right now I'm the stranger who borrowed one of your horses when mine went lame with a cut frog. You're worried about getting yours back. You've come after it. Now do exactly as I say or we're both dead!''

Recovering from his confusion, Oss nodded. "I get it." He glanced toward the shed. "You're sure you know who did it?"

"Dead sure! And I think I know how we can trap him. Have Henry and the rest wait up for me. If I don't show, something's gone wrong, but don't come looking. Don't!''

Oss glanced past him. "Somebody's coming," he whispered.

Clayt turned to see Jake Harmer heading toward them, and he was looking for trouble. Turning back to Oss, Clayt spoke in a loud, unfriendly voice. "I told you, mister, I'd get your horse back as soon as I could. I just hired on here. I was fixing to bring it soon to see if mine's alright now."

When Harmer reached them Clayt nodded toward Oss. "He's from Red Creek. I borrowed his horse and he thinks I forgot to return it."

Oss swung down from the saddle. "I didn't say you stole it—if that's what you're saying. I didn't come looking for trouble. We've had enough of that. The horse you borrowed is harness-broke, too. We need it when you can spare it."

"Why didn't you bring my horse with you?" Clayt challenged.

Oss thought fast. "His frog was bad cut. I figured if you'd found work you could ride a ranch horse and let me take mine."

Harmer bumped Clayt's arm. "Give 'im his broken-down plug, Clayton, and git him outta here."

"I only want him back if you're done using him," Oss explained mildly. "You can keep him for another week or more if you need him."

Harmer spat a stream of tobacco juice with unerring accuracy. It missed Oss' boot by an inch. "We're not so damned hard up around here," he growled, "that we gotta put our hands up on spavined plough horses. We don't want no trouble with neighbors. You go git your horse and hit the trail, mister." He jerked his head toward the corral. "Ride on down there and pick him up. An' keep sumpthin' in mind, too—we don't hire hands that takes things and fergits t' return 'em."

At the corral Harmer watched while Clayt handed over the halter lead on his horse. Oss did a credible job of playing his role. "I thank you, mister. We'll keep your horse until it's well then bring it to you."

"Never mind comin' here agin," Harmer snapped. "My boys'll pick him up next trip to Vegas."

"Thank you, sir," Oss replied. "We try to be friendly neighbors, too."

Clayt watched until he had passed through the main gate then returned to his work. A few minutes later Harmer walked up. "Is he the one you talked to before?"

"...and his father, I think it was," Clayt replied. Harmer spat in disgust and sauntered off.

For the remainder of the day Clayt concentrated on his repair work. Several times he grew aware that Harmer was watching him, studying him, really. Shortly before quitting time, he came by.

"I noticed sumpthin'," he said. "I noticed, like you, the sodbuster don't carry no Colt, an' he had a Henry in a saddle boot like yourn."

Strung tight in anticipation of his night ride, Clayt found it difficult to appear casual. "Not everybody favors a six-gun," he replied. "I know a lot of men who would rather work with a rifle—a repeater, that is—even close in."

"Some would, I guess," Harmer agreed, "but I noticed his rifle boot too. It's the same as yourn."

Clayt turned to him with a cold, level gaze.

"If you know anything about Indian work, you should recognize it, Harmer. There are probably a thousand of them in the Plains country."

The foreman ducked his head in conditional agreement. "S'possible. But there's one more thing that needs answerin'."

Clayt dropped his tools so abruptly that Harmer's right arm jerked toward his Colt. "I want to know two things right now, Jake. What's this 'one more thing,' and what are you getting at?"

Harmer managed a wan smile. "Now don't go gittin' hot. When a man's pickin' a partner fur a dangerous job, he's got a right t'ease his mind some."

"Well, ease it, then," Clayt replied. "You talk straight and so will I. What's this one more thing?"

"Prob'ly aint nuthin' much, but I noticed you an' that sodbuster talk the same way, sorta."

Clayt knew that Harmer's observation was correct.

"I understand," he said, "that those people came from the South after the war. I told you where my people came from. Everybody from that part of the country talks pretty much the same way—and most people don't lost their born accents, anymore than Texas folks or Kansas flatlanders do. You can't make anything more out of it than that, so don't waste your time."

Harmer's eyes hardened, then he seemed to ease. "That figgers, I guess. Anyways, when I note things, I like to find out about 'em. That's how I've stayed out of a burial blanket this long."

The hours dragged by. Clayt had considered plans for getting away from the ranch on one pretext or another and had abandoned them all. Now a new horse added to his problem. The girl had taken the buckskin mare that seemed to have adopted him. There's a curious chemistry between a horse and a rider and while he did not understand it, Clayt was acutely aware of it. The closeness of the relationship could spell the difference between life and death in the territory. A good horse often could sense approaching danger sooner and faster than the rider. That's why he had given the girl the buckskin mare.

There were a dozen horses in the ranch's *caballada*. There was one big chestnut gelding that he had considered first. It was skittish at times, but not particularly so around him when he was in the corral. The biggest trouble he would have would be getting there unseen and getting a saddle on the animal.

When the lamp went out in Harmer's cabin, he waited an hour. There was only a sliver of waning moon. That would help. A sudden dangerous oversight jolted him. He had meant to stash his Winchester in the shed in case some of the boys happened to see him going with it. Without it he could pretend to be going to the outhouse.

It was after nine o'clock when he decided to make his try. Pleading weariness, he had cut short the usual pointless palaver with Tanner. When the old trail boss turned his face to the wall and soon began his familiar snoring, Clayt picked up his rifle and boots and made for the shed. Once inside, he brushed off his socks and got into his boots. A minute later his saddle and saddle blanket were resting atop the corral rail.

Carrying the bridle over his arm, he moved quietly among the horses until he found the chestnut. When he reached to give it a reassuring pat, it tossed its head and sidestepped. "Easy, boy...easy..." he whispered. It took several tries before the gelding accepted the bit. As he started to lead him to the fence, one of the other animals whinnyed. Clayt held his breath for a long moment then saddled up.

Unwilling to take a chance on mounting in the corral, Clayt led the gelding several hundred yards up the road. When he put his foot in the stirrup, his left hand on the horn with the reins bunched, and his right on the cantle, the animal took a short step forward and swung him into the saddle.

For ten minutes he held him to a fast walk. When he was safely out of hearing, he urged the long-legged gelding into a ground-covering lope.

An hour later the sound of a lone rider passing caused Manuel Santos to lift up from his shambled bed.

"Qué pasa?" he whispered.

"Quién sabe," his wife replied.

He listened a moment longer then sat up. Very seldom did late riders pass Tres Dedos. When they did they were usually hands from the Gavilan who had been spending their pay gold in the store and the saloon in Las Vegas.

"Tal vez un hombre de Gavilan," he said, *"Pero porqué tan tarde?"*

Rosita did not reply. He listened a moment longer, then rose and peered into the night. One of the horses in his corral had whinnyed softly but the rider had gone on out of earshot. Nothing could be heard or seen. A candle left on the crude table was guttering. He blew it out and returned to the bed.

Jake Harmer sat on the edge of his bunk studying the explosives he had prepared earlier. To be effective and still allow reasonable time to get away, the fuses would have to be carefully timed and cut to length. The more he worried over the fuses, the more uncertain he was. To be extra sure, he decided to recheck the burn time on the longest fuse. The roll of spare fuse was on the bench in the shed. Checking to make certain he had his knife and a block of phosphorus matches, he picked up the lantern and went out.

It took only a few minutes to measure out a long length of fuse from the spare roll. As he was about to leave, an empty saddle rack caught his eye. Curious, he paused to check and found that Clayton's saddle and bridle were missing.

Puzzled, he went to the corral and looked to see if perhaps they were still on the rail. There was no sign of them. Frowning, he stood for a moment. If a saddle was missing a horse would be, too.

Carrying the lantern, he entered the corral and began looking at the animals. Even in the dark it took him only seconds to discover that the big chestnut was missing. Hurrying, he carried the lantern low to check tracks. The signs were easy to read. The gelding had been led by the reins.

"Why in hell would that fool ride out at night?" he asked himself aloud. An instant later he answered his own question. "He don't want to do the Red Crick job!" But the answer didn't make any sense. Clayton had seemed more than willing to help. Turning, he started back toward the corral and a sudden thought stopped him. Something about the encounter with the rider from the settlement who had come about the borrowed horse made him very uneasy. He couldn't put a finger on it, but something was wrong.

"I wonder," he said aloud, "if Clayton and that sodbuster are hooked up somehow? I...just...wonder...." Acting on an impulse, he ran back to the corral, saddled his own mount, and rode it to the cabin to get his guns.

"That high-an'-mighty dude can't have much lead on me," he breathed as he spurred to a gallop from a standing start.

"I'm damned well gonna do me a little findin' out!"

At the Santos adobe he jumped from the saddle and pounded on the door. "Git outta that bed, *hombre*! It's Jake Harmer. I want'a talk to ya!"

He heard the sound of a sleepy woman's voice complaining.

"Git out here, Santos. Pronto!"

He was about to bang on the door again, when it squeaked open and the Mexican stood there holding a candle in one hand and his pants bunched at the waist in the other.

"Listen to me!" he shouted in the man's face. "Did a rider go by here a little bit ago?"

"*Si, señor*. I hear one horse—*para el norte*."

"When?" Harmer barked.

Santos shrugged. "Maybe one hour."

"Did you see who it was?"

"*No, señor*, I was sleeping."

"You were asleep but you heard him. You're lyin', Santos!"

"*No, señor₁ Es la verdad.*"

"If yur lyin', Santos, you'll be a dead *choclo!*"

"*Señor*, when I hear the noise, I wake up. My horses make noise, too."

"Did you look out?"

"*Si*. It was much dark. I see nothing."

"The hell there wasn't!" Santos recoiled as Harmer all but spit the words in his face. "That was my new man. He's gone and sneaked off and stole one of my horses. I'll kill the horse thief!"

He remounted and spurred his lathered mount to a jump-away start.

It was nearing one in the morning when Clayt reached Red Creek. He tied the big chestnut to a piñon and scrambled down the trail on foot.

Oss and Henry Deyer and a half dozen other men were waiting in his father's house. His mother and Nelda ran to him, their eyes moist with tears of relief. "Thank God," Mary breathed as she held him. "We all thought you'd never come back." Nelda clung to his arm in a wordless greeting then pointed to Kate. "Thank you, Clayt, for sending Katie to us." She reached up and smoothed her palm against his cheek. "Thank you so much. She's a blessing!"

Clayt looked at the girl who was standing behind them. It was the first time he had heard her name. "Kate, is it? I did some honest-to-God praying for you, girl. I'm sure glad you made it!" He looked at her closely and the change was miraculous. In the soft lantern light, dressed in one of his sister's flannel wrappers, she was more than just plain pretty. Kate Williams made no response. It was the first time that she had seen him clearly. What she had felt the night before when he had hidden her from Oakley was much more than just gratitude. Some of it was the secure feeling in his arms and the tenderness as he had pressed her cheek against his shoulder, feelings that were borne out now in his voice and by his appearance. She wanted to speak of gratitude. They were the only words she would be able to find now. The rest was just feeling, and there were no words.

Clayt continued to study Kate for a long moment, then turned to Henry.

"We've got to talk right now," he said. "If I don't get back before I'm missed ..." Deliberately, he did not finish the thought.

Henry Deyer glanced at the unaccustomed gun belt and the forty-four. Their simple presence spoke of more danger than Clayt would ever admit. "What do you want us to do," he asked, "to help get this man?"

While they listened, not without grave misgivings on the part of his mother and sister and Kate, Clayt outlined the only plan he felt stood a ghost of a chance of delivering Harmer, and later Oakley, into their hands.

When he had finished, Henry turned to the others.

"We've got to make this work! There is no other way. We're going to do exactly what Clayt says, no matter what the cost."

Mary came to Clayt and held his hand. "When will you be back?"

"We'll reach the rim about midnight tomorrow," he said with more assurance than he felt. Turning to Henry, he added, "...and if I'm not with him, and Harmer shows up, gun him down, Henry! Don't give him any more chance than he gave us."

As he turned to leave he said, "I could use a prayer or two. Miracles happen. Ask Kate!"

Oss followed him outside. "Take my horse to the top, Clayt. Tie him. I'll get him in the morning."

"Can't take the time," Clayt called back as he sprinted over the dam top and headed for the foot of the trail. Driving himself, he reached the rim in ten minutes. Panting from the exertion, he looked for the chestnut. It was not there, not where he'd left it. The realization sent a shock through him.

Before he could think, Harmer rode out of the cover with his Colt drawn.

"Git yur hands up—high, real high—and keep 'em there!" he snarled. "I oughta be locked in the crazy house fur b'lievin' an artistic liar like you!" He moved to point-blank range. "If you wanta see the sun come up, you mizz'able skunk, you'd better start tellin' a mighty good story or I'm gonna bore a big damn hole right through that fancy head of yourn!"

The shortness of breath helped Clayt conceal his shock.

"Put that gun down, you damned fool," he gasped. "If you had any brains, Harmer, you'd know there isn't enough gold in Oakley's safe to make me go down there without first being sure we have a chance to get out alive." He nodded toward the trail head. "It's a damn good think for you and me that I decided to look first. Those people may be crazy but they're not stupid. What makes you think they'd leave the place unprotected after what happened?"

Shock had given way to anger now and his voice was under better control. "If we'd gone down there tomorrow night, neither of us would have come out alive." He aimed a finger at the foreman who still kept the gun aimed at his head.

"Instead of shooting me and having a swarm of men on your tail in ten minutes, you'd better thank God—*and* me—that I did sneak down there."

When Harmer made no response, Clayt pressed his advantage.

"They've got a guard at the bottom day and night, and a half dozen others must be taking turns waiting at the top. There's only one chance and now I know how to handle it."

Still holding his Colt, but lower now, Harmer jutted his face down at Clayt.

"How do I know you ain't lyin'?" he demanded.

"You don't, Harmer, so why don't you go tippy-toeing down there like I just did and find out? Go on. Do it! I'm too old to be a young fool and too young to be a dead one. Go on, Harmer. I'll wait right here."

"You was a fool to do it," Harmer countered. Pointing to the trail head with his six-gun, he added, "How many men have they got standin' watch?"

"As far as I could tell from where I could get without being caught, they've got one standing down the trail about twenty yards behind some cover. They probably have one at the bottom, too. I know for sure there's one at the top. I hid while they changed the midnight watch."

Reluctantly, Harmer returned the Colt to its holster. He knew he needed help and Clayton had been down there in daylight. If he bungled the job this time he'd be finished with Oakley. He could probably get on with John Chism at South Spring again but the work was not nearly as good as at the Gavilan spread.

Harmer dismounted and stretched. "How come ya didn't let on that ya wanted to go scoutin' in the first place?"

"I was going whether you liked it or not, Harmer. It's my hide and I don't ask anybody's permission to keep it whole."

The foreman continued to wrestle with doubt. Finally he eased and leaned against his horse. "All right, let's git on back and figger out how we kin handle the ones that's settin' up waitin' fur us."

"I've got that worked out," Clayt replied, "but it's going to take both of us to do it—and we might have to forget putting a charge on the far side of the dam. Too near the houses. If we light even a long fuse and anybody sees it burning, we might have to shoot our way out." Remounting, he said, "Let's get back."

Both riders and their mounts were worn and the sun's rays had already begun to slant through the low places in the dark silhouette of hills to the east. They turned their horses into the corral and headed for the cookshack.

Oakley had been standing on the veranda having his first coffee when he saw them ride in. He set the mug aside and crossed the yard.

Calling from the door, he said, "I want to see you, Jake."

The foreman freed his legs from under the table.

"Yes sir?"

"What were you and Clayton doing riding in all wore out at sunup? Where did you go?"

Harmer glanced at Clayton who seemed not to have heard.

"I wanted to scout Red Crick again. Good thing I did. They got guards on the dam now."

In a voice edged with sarcasm, Oakley said, "It takes real brains to figure that out, don't it?"

Harmer looked crestfallen. "Well, T.K....uh...what I really wanted t'figger out was how to git rid of 'em real quiet so we kin plant the charges."

"Did you come up with something?"

"Yes sir. I've got it figgered real good." Oakley walked over to the table and stood opposite Clayt.

"Did you hear what Jake said?"

"Sorry," Clayt replied. "I wasn't paying attention to anything but this." He tapped scrambled eggs and a slab of ham with his knife. Oakley knew better and smiled.

"Jake says he's got things figured out. Do you agree?"

Clayt pretended to be considering his answer. After a short silence, he nodded. "We'll get done what has to be done."

"Good," Oakley replied. Then, speaking pointedly to Harmer, he added, "And for your sake, Jake, I hope you're both right."

"Don't worry none, T.K.," the foreman replied, struggling to keep the persistent doubt from his voice, "We'll git to it t'night and bring it off jes' like ya planned."

"Just like *you* planned," Oakley corrected. "I didn't tell you how...." His sudden smile chilled Harmer. "I just told you where—and when."

Clayt smiled to himself. There it was again—another admission that was also a confession—and this time from the superintendent himself!

Chapter Ten

Jake Harmer and Clayton Adams slept in until noon. In midafternoon, they rode to the nearby flood wash and tested the burning time on the fuses. Using approximate distances, they rehearsed their strategy until they were satisfied.

At sundown, T.K. Oakley came to the corral. Ignoring Harmer, he said, "You do this job right, Clayton, there'll be better work for you. I'm going to need smart hands when we start driving north to the railroad next spring. Prove out and like I said, you've got a good future here."

Clayt managed a smile. "That's the second time you've said that. I guess you must mean it."

The superintendent's long, angular face hardened for a moment, then he matched Clayt's smile.

"I always do. I'll be looking for both of you around sunup. If the water comes through, Clayton, you'll be able to buy that big chestnut you seem to favor now." He nodded at Harmer. "You might even have enough left over to ride to Vegas and get rigged out fancy like Jake." His smile faded, "If you're stupid enough."

Nursing his resentment, Jake Harmer rode north on the Las Vegas road with Clayt. Something about this new hand still troubled him. It wasn't so much the man's unexpected skill with the Winchester and six-gun. The uneasiness had started from the very beginning at Tres Dedos. But there was more to it than that. There was something threatening in the man's quiet self-possession and in the mystery of his early years.

Clayt glanced over at him and Harmer's preoccupied expression made him smile inwardly.

It was shortly after ten o'clock when they reined in at the top of the trail and turned their horses into the dense growth of bushy piñon trees. Jake Harmer glanced around uneasily as he dismounted. With elaborate unconcern he probed here and there, looking. When he saw Clayt watching him he said, "Just wanta poke around a little—make sure this is the best place t'leave the horses."

He shouldered his way through the thick cover and Clayt could make out that he was stooping to examine something. He had dumped the bodies of the two gunslingers there. It was obvious that he was looking for signs. In the darkness he wouldn't find any. The men had buried the bodies carefully to discourage prowling animals. When he returned, Clayt asked, "Find what you were looking for?"

"Just studyin'," Harmer replied with his back turned.

Clayt walked to his horse and removed the explosives from his saddlebag. Harmer took the rest of them and tied the two small cans of black powder from which he had improvised hand bombs and fastened them to his gun belt. Clayt unbuttoned his shirt and slipped the dynamite sticks inside. Snugging his rifle under his arm, he moved from the cover to the trail head.

"I'm going down and get the first lookout. Then I'll see if I can locate another one."

"Yer gonna make a hell of a lot of noise doin' that," Harmer warned.

"I'll get it done," Clayt promised, "and it will be done with no shooting and no knifing. There's going to be no killing this time. We agreed on that."

Struggling to control his nervousness, Harmer replied, "I know, an' I was a damned fool. I still think what we oughta do is just go in shootin', surprise 'em, short fuse the spillway, and git the hell outa there before they know what's hit 'em. If some gits kilt in the explosions, we never figgered it thata way." He shook a finger at Clayt. "You know damn good and well they're gonna ride up after us anyhow."

Clayt turned and walked a step toward him. "You change things now, Harmer, and I'm riding. We won't have a chance!"

Before the foreman could argue, he disappeared down the trail.

Clayt reached the bottom quickly. A soft night-bird call brought Oss out.

"Thank God you made it. Where's Harmer?"

"Up top waiting for me to fetch that body I promised. Where are the others?"

"Two men are below the dam with shotguns. You passed right by two more. They're hiding along the edge of the trail."

"Good," Clayt said. His voice echoed the relief he felt. "Let's get on with it."

They hurried across the dam to the Deyer house. Henry was waiting for them. Oss seated himself and tapped his forehead.

"All right, Pop, do your scratching."

The older man wiped the point of a skinning knife on a damp cloth and held his son's temple taut under a calloused thumb. Quickly, he drew the point diagonally down from Oss' hairline to the corner of his eyebrow.

"Make it bleed good, Pop. It don't hurt. It only sort of stings."

"It's bleeding plenty," his father replied.

"Enough to smear me up good?"

"There's more than enough," Clayt assured him. "Now, let's ditch this dynamite and get it over with."

He slipped the fused explosives from his shirt and handed them to Henry. He and Oss left then. Ten minutes later Clayt reappeared at the head of the trail.

"It's done," he said to Harmer. "There was only one. He's out. Help me get him up here."

They found Oss sprawled on his back. Harmer jammed a filthy bandana in his mouth for a gag while Clayt removed two rawhide thongs from his pocket and bound his friend's hands and ankles with slip knots deliberately tied to be loosened.

Together they picked up Oss' limp body and hauled him up to the piñons.

"Lean him against this tree," Clayt said. When he saw Harmer fingering the leather bound handle protruding from the left side of his belt, he snapped, "Leave that blade where it is, Jake! He's not going to come to for a half hour yet, and if he does he's not going anywhere and he's not going to say anything."

Unhappy, the foreman relaxed. "With his throat cut, he sure as hell ain't goin' nowhere," he grumbled.

Clayt rose. "Quit jabbering, for God's sake, and let's get on with it!"

At the near end of the dam, they could see the flood control gate box.

"Get into it, Jake. I'll take care of the other end."

"You got plenty of matches?" he asked.

"Plenty. Now get in and keep down. I'll set the charges and light them. Don't you get jumpy and light yours until I get back here. Somebody might be up late. If you see any lights come up in windows, or any lanterns moving outside, stay down. I'll be able to see them, too, and I'll stay put until they've gone." He started to leave and stopped. "Remember, don't light your charges until I get back. You'll see my matches. When you do, I'll be coming fast. That's when you light off—and not before. Don't make a mistake. Wait!"

Before he had gone ten feet, Clayt was a vanishing shape in the canyon's deep darkness. Harmer pressed his fist against his middle to relieve the unaccustomed tightness. Silently, he damned himself for letting Clayton do all of the planning even though he understood that he himself was better suited to the head-on tactic of direct assault he had learned with Quantrill.

At the far end flood gate, Clayton found Henry Deyer waiting with Vic Bodine. Both were armed with powerful ten-gauge shotguns.

"Let's go over this again," he said. "When I light my matches Harmer will think I've lit the fuse. He won't try to light his until I get back in the gate box with him. He won't get a chance because I'll bash his stupid head."

"When I'm sure he's out, I'll fire one shot. You fire your signal to the men and close in fast. If it all works, we'll have our man." He paused. "If I have to, I'll break my promise and kill him and do my worrying about consequences later."

Henry Deyer reached out and gave Clayt's arm an encouraging squeeze. "Light up, Clayt, and God help us!"

Crouched in the shelter of the gate box, Jake Harmer stared tensely, watching for the match flare. After what seemed an eternity, he saw it. The flare was followed by the heavy thud of running boots. He was in the act of moving aside to make room for Clayt when the rattle of heavy boards reached him. Immediately the footsteps ceased and he heard a muffled groan.

Henry Deyer and Vic Bodine heard it too.

"Something's happened to him," Henry said in an anxious whisper. "Let's hold it a minute longer." When everything on the dam top remained ominously silent, he said, "Clayt's got trouble! I'm going out there!" Ignoring Bodine's protest, he crouched and ran. He had gone only a few yards when he found Clayt struggling to drag himself back. "Hurt my leg!" he gasped.

In the gate box Jake Harmer was close to panic. The charge should be about ready to blow. Where in hell was Clayton?

Henry kneeled down close. "What happened, Clayt?"

"I stumbled over those planks. I can't get back to Harmer!"

Hidden behind a boulder near the foot of the trail, Oss also realized something had gone wrong. He had seen Clayt's matches flare and had waited tensely for the revolver report from the gate box and Henry's answering signal.

When it didn't come he fingered the trigger of his own shotgun and tried to keep a hold on himself. He hoped the others waiting on the trail higher up would understand, too, and wait.

Still kneeling beside Clayt, Henry Deyer saw the hopelessness of reviving the plan. "We can't let that murdering animal get away," he said. Before Clayt realized what he was about to do, the older man raised the shotgun and fired it into the air.

"For good God's sake, Henry," Clayt shouted, "don't charge him! You haven't got a chance now!"

Jake Harmer froze as he recognized Clayt's voice. Realizing that he had been led into a hopeless trap, he let out a wild scream of rage and began blazing away indiscriminately.

Henry Deyer flattened against Clayt to protect him and reloaded his ten-gauge.

Screaming curses now, Harmer emptied his Colt. Shielded behind the heavy planks, he was reloading when Oss called out from the cover of a boulder above and behind him. "Drop your guns! You're trapped! There's twenty men here looking for an excuse to kill you! Drop them, Harmer! You're finished!"

Harmer felt his gun belt. It held thirty-one rounds.

"Come an' git me, ya mizzable, water hoggin' hay shakers!" Twisting in the box, he emptied a second cylinder of shots randomly scattered in the direction of the voice. They slammed into the face of the boulder and into the cliff behind Oss, sprinkling him with sandstone dust.

Shouting, in the hope that Henry and Clayt would hear him out on the dam, he warned, "Keep him pinned down! We're closing in on him from the trail!" His own voice echoed back from the canyon walls.

Henry Deyer, still flat next to Clayt, whispered, "Can you get yourself back there? I'm going to crawl some closer and blast him a time or two."

"He'll see your muzzle flash, Henry! You'll be a sitting duck! Don't try it!" Vic Bodine echoed the warning.

"I'll get below the dam face. I can get a toehold on the stones. He can't get a clean shot and we can keep him wasting ammunition."

The silence from the flood gate meant Harmer was reloading. As he crawled back toward the west bank of Red Creek, Clayt tried to estimate how many rounds Harmer had wasted. Twelve, for sure. That meant he would have at least four more full loads, plus his rifle. They'd have to chance it and keep him shooting. He couldn't set off his own dynamite charges without blowing himself to hell. Oss seemed cool. He had proved he could be when he blundered into a confrontation with Harmer at the Gavilan.

Before Clayt and Bodine could reach the safety of the other end of the dam, Henry's ten-gauge shotgun shattered the silence. Instantly, Harmer fired where he had seen the flash. When there was no answering shot, he clamped his lips in grim satisfaction. "I got one of 'em," he thought.

His answer was another blast from the same position. Frustrated, he fired three more rounds. The last one struck a rock and went whining off into the night.

The echos were still dying out between the canyon walls

when another heavy shotgun blast came from above and
behind him. Twisting in the uncomfortable confinement of
the box, he got off the remaining two rounds at a supposed
target, and reloaded.

Oss called out again. "We're counting your rounds, Harmer. You better start counting your minutes! You don't have
many of either left. Give up, you damned fool! Throw your
Colt and your Winchester into the pond. We know what
you've got. Give up and you won't be killed. You'll be taken
to the law for a fair trial. We don't want to kill you, Harmer,
but we will if you make us!"

Jake Harmer knew the voice was coming from behind good
cover—far better than his. He realized too, that even if he
conserved his ammunition, his time would soon be up. He
felt the reassuring weight of the two small black-powder hand
bombs hanging on his belt. They were his only chance of
getting to the trail alive, and he could only manage that slim
chance if he could keep them pinned down—and that cost
rounds. They knew he had a Colt and a Winchester. Clayton
knew that, too. Curses at himself, his own stupidity, mingled
with the others.

"Ya want me, ya come an' git me!" he shouted. "Let's
see jes' how brave y'are! Dirty, sneaky, chicken-livered
sodbusters—wud'nt give a man a chance!"

Holding his sprained leg, Clayt's mind raced. Both sides
were pinned down. The only thing they could do was keep
him wasting ammunition and hope that they had judged his
supply correctly.

Almost simultaneously, two ten-gauge shots blasted the
box, one from Henry Deyer's weapon and another from Oss'.
With insane recklessness, Harmer spent rounds in answering
fire, and both men smiled grimly and reloaded. In a cross
fire, Harmer knew he could lose his last gamble.

Two more clusters of buckshot slammed into his hiding
place but he did not answer their fire. In a minute he'd need

all of his Colt rounds. The Winchester would have to be left behind. He slipped the six-shooter into its holster and loosened the two small black-powder bombs. Their fuses would ignite the explosive in ten seconds.

He estimated the distance to the men hiding behind him and to those who were still out on the dam. No use wasting a charge on them. Escape was the other way. The man who had been shouting and shooting above and behind was out of throwing range. His only chance would be to steal from his cover, crawl close enough, light both fuses, heave them, and shoot his way to the foot of the trail. Once there, he'd try to outrun them to the top and get to his horse.

For several nerve-racking minutes the only sounds in Red Creek Canyon were the familiar ones, the soft rush of water over the spillway, the occasional calls of a night bird, and the hollow, metalic clang of cowbells coming from the pasture downstream.

Harmer could feel the pulse throbbing in his neck as he leaned to check the short fuses. The block of phosphorus matches was in his shirt pocket. He pulled it out and broke off four. Once out on the dam, if he took time to light both fuses, the flare would give him away. Half sick and soaked with anxious sweat, he decided to leave one behind rather than risk a flesh-riddling cluster of buckshot.

Holding the matches in his mouth, he eased over the edge of his protective planking and flattened against the earthen dam. Inching along, he propelled himself with his left forearm to stay as low as possible. The hand bomb was clutched under his arm and the Colt was ready in his hand. If he could make it half the distance from the flood gate to the foot of the trail he'd be within throwing distance.

He stopped twice, afraid that the scrape of his boots as he pushed would give him away. Just then, the long silence was shattered by a buckshot blast just a few yards above him and he heard Oss' voice again.

"I hope you're thinking it out, Harmer. You can't get out of here. Give up. You'll get fair treatment. You'll get the chance you didn't give our people—fourteen of them—dead! Give up, Harmer, or we're coming for you!"

Again, no answer, only the ominous silence. From behind his cover, Oss peered into the darkness. He could just barely make out the squat, square shape of the floodgate housing. On the far side of the dam, the houses were still obscured in the deeper shadows of the west canyon wall.

He turned to John Bates who was crouching beside him. "What do you think he's up to?" he whispered.

"I don't think we could hit him in there," Bates answered. "...an' I don't hardly think he's used up his loads. There's been no rifle fire yet."

Oss knew that, too, and it worried him. "The only thing is," he replied, "to use it, he's got to show more of himself for a target. We might get lucky, but we want him alive."

Unseen on the dam top, Harmer positioned himself to take his last chance for escape. His mouth was cottony dry and his hands were slippery with dirty sweat. Breathing like a cornered animal, he gathered his legs under him, took the matches from his mouth, struck them, and touched them to the fuse.

The instant it started to splutter, he jumped up, took aim, and threw it toward the place he thought his tormentor was hiding. Flattening again, he stoppered his ears and waited.

When Oss saw the trail of sparks arcing in his direction, he froze for an instant, then shouted to John Bates to get down. Pressing himself against the boulder, he covered his face. Seconds later a two-pound can of black powder exploded at the base of his hiding place. The shock deafened him momentarily and both men were showered with bits of rock.

Harmer charged at the base of the trail with his Colt blazing away at unseen attackers. When Oss realized what was happening, he yelled, "He's trying to blast his way out of here!" Leaving his cover, he rushed to the trail in time to make out Harmer's indistinct figure driving up the steep slope. Shouting a second warning to the men concealed along the lower end of the trail, Oss aimed the heavy shotgun from his hip and pulled the trigger. Harmer stumbled and sharp bits of rock bit into the palm of his left hand. The heavy load of buckshot shredded some scrub brush not two feet away.

His breath exploded in lung-searing gasps as he redoubled his effort to outclimb the man behind him. Another, lighter shotgun blast slammed into his ears ahead of him and a bit to his right. When that load went wide, too, a glimmer of hope gave him renewed strength.

Oss had to slow to reload and lost several yards. He heard rather than saw the running figure. Taking time to aim, he pulled the trigger and in an instant Harmer's sharp outcry reached him. A nettle sting of nearly spent pellets had struck him in the back. He knew he was bleeding but he continued to drive himself like a madman.

Oss shouted at him again. "We're waiting for you up top, too, Harmer. Give up!" With no breath to waste on retorts, he forced himself to keep scrambling. If he could last another few yards he would make it to the rim and freedom.

The hornet sting of another blast made him cry out, but he kept going. Ahead and a little above, he could make out the dark shapes of the piñons. In a superhuman effort he stumbled to them and let out a cry of relief when he saw the animals. Staggering, he reached his horse, pulled the reins free, and grasped the saddle horn.

Summoning the last ounce of strength born of hope, he jammed his left boot in the stirrup and started to pull himself up. Suddenly the deliberately loosened saddle slipped forward and came off. As he fell backwards with the saddle on top of him, his Colt slipped free of the holster.

From out of nowhere four men appeared. Jakob Gruen put the barrel of his shotgun against Harmer's temple.

"I'd risk going to hell to kill you," he said, "if I wasn't afraid I'd meet you there! Don't you make a move or I'll take that chance!"

Fighting for breath, Oss came up. For a long moment he stood looking down at Harmer. "We'll be finished with you in a bit," he said between breaths. "You make a wrong move and you're dead."

Harmer's eyes swung wildly from one to the other of men whose faces he could scarcely make out in the dark. He knew his Colt was missing. Out of the corner of his eye he could see it lying within reach. As he made a dive for it, Oss swung around and smashed the heavy barrel of his shotgun into the side of Harmer's head. His knees buckled and he went down.

Trussed up, they draped his unconscious body over his horse. A half hour later, in the soot-dimmed glow of their lanterns, the settlers watched as the man who had brought unspeakable tragedy on them was carried into the small adobe strong house that would be his prison until he confessed and could be taken to Las Vegas and the law.

In the meeting house, tall, gaunt John Stark spoke to Henry Deyer who had asked them to gather there.

"I know what Asa wanted," he said in a voice still dulled by grief, "but there ain't no law there now, you say. And even if there was, it's common talk that nobody in the territory gets justice against the railroads and the cattlemen who ship with them. If we take the man to the law, it could go hard with us and we'd be forced out anyhow."

Henry Deyer listened patiently, then nodded.

"I know, John. There's always such talk. Ever since the

'fifties and gold in California, more and more family folks are coming west. When that happens the law always comes with them. Asa was right and we'll keep to his wishes.''

"What if you can't get the man to admit anything?" Stark asked, "even if in God's eyes we know it's the truth?"

"During the war, John, you know we had certain sure ways to make prisoners talk. We'll not be wasting much time on this one. I promise you, he'll talk!"

Trying not to limp, Clayt came in and joined Henry.

"I want to say something. We owe Harmer's capture to Oss. When I went down and couldn't keep to our plan, Oss stepped in and did the best that anyone could do—and we've got Harmer, alive. We can all thank God and Oss for that."

A murmur of gratitude ran through the settlers.

"I know," he continued, "that Harmer's boss ordered him to blow up the dam. I don't know for sure whether he ordered killing. We'll find that out, too. And we'll find out if the new owners had a hand in it. Whoever did will pay." He lifted a cautioning finger. "When Harmer and I don't come riding in by sunup, or a little later, Oakley is going to send somebody to see what the trouble was, especially if he doesn't see more water coming downstream. We've got two of his horses now. They've got to be kept out of sight in the barn." He nodded at Kate who was sitting with his mother and sister.

"The girl's got to be kept out of sight until this is settled. Oakley had a special interest in this little lady."

Henry Deyer reached over and rested a hand on Clayt's arm. "And you've got to stay out of sight, too. If they come looking and Oakley is with them, it's best you're not seen."

"We'll clean up the spent shells and things so it'll look like nothing happened down here. Oakley himself is not likely to come down looking, but he might send one of his men down to ask around. We want to have him leave wondering.'' He looked at the weary faces. "That's all. You can rest now.''

As they rose, Nelda took Kate's hand and led her to Clayt. "My dear brother, Kate and I are going to ease that knee with hot cloths and arnica''—she glanced at Oss's forehead and the alarming smear of dried blood—"after we patch up my husband-to-be because you used him for cut bait.''

Clayt slipped an arm around his sister and took Kate's hand. "Sure a clumsy fool with two left feet deserves patching up?''

Nelda gave Kate a questioning look. "What do you think?''

Kate lowered her eyes and her fingers tightened around Clayt's. In a barely audible voice, she said, "I think I'm the luckiest person born—no matter how many left feet he has.''

Chapter Eleven

T.K. Oakley grimaced as he tasted the coffee he had warmed over from the night before. He glanced at the cookhouse and saw smoke from a newly lit fire curling up from the chimney. Tucking in his shirttails as he went, he crossed to the bunkhouse and peered in. Buck Tanner, in the midst of a huge yawn, was seated on the edge of his bedding. When he saw the superintendent in the doorway, he straightened and got up.

"Mornin', T.K."

Ignoring the greeting, Oakley aimed a finger at Clayt's empty bunk. "Did he come in last night?"

"No sir—'less he come in and went agin' 'tween the time I went to sleep and woke up...jus' now...."

Oakley's response was a grunt. He turned away and paused just outside the door.

"Before you eat, check Jake's bunk, then come over to the house."

"Yes sir," Buck replied. "Be there in two shakes."

As he left he saw the cook come out of the cookshack carrying a large pot of coffee. Buck Tanner smiled. Half to himself, he said, "Guess ole' T.K.'s missin' havin' a lotta handy things done fur him now that the girl's flew off."

He passed the cook coming back empty-handed. The Mexican *cocinero* scowled. *"Siempre lo mismo! Mas trabajo.*

Mas trabajo," he grumbled. The old man grinned. "Ya come here lookin' fur work, amigo. A little more now an' then won't hurt ya none."

The door to the main room was open. Peering through as he knocked, he saw Oakley pouring two cups of fresh coffee.

"Come and get yours," he called. "I want to talk to you." The superintendent indicated a chair.

"Jake and Clayton rode out last night to finish off the job at Red Creek. They should have been back here well before sunup. Jake's bunk was not mussed either, was it?"

"Didn't look slept in to me."

Oakley nodded and regarded his coffee mug thoughtfully. After another sip he looked up.

"If they don't show by noon, I've got to know what happened. I believe Jake is dumb enough to rope his own hind leg but I don't think that Clayton fellow is."

Buck Tanner could guess what was coming. The wait was not long. Oakley took several more sips at his coffee then set it aside. Studying the old hand carefully, he said, "Have you been up to Red Creek? Do you know the lay of the place?"

Buck Tanner blotted his drooping moustache with the back of his hand. "When they was first settlin' there, I rode by a time or two—cut off from the Vegas road—jes outa curiosity."

"Did you ever ride down and talk to them?"

"Never did. Didn't seem like p'ticular friendly folks."

"Did they see you—I mean were any of them riding around up top when you came by?"

"Not that I saw."

Oakley toyed with the handle of the mug for a moment.

"In other words, if you rode over to do a little looking around and you ran into any of them, you think they wouldn't know you?"

Buck shook his head. "No sir. Not if I didn't want 'em to."

Bracing his hands on the kitchen table, Oakley got up.

"Alright, Buck, there'll be extra gold on payday if you can go up there and get me some idea of what happened."

"I kin do that alright, I reckon, T.K.... But what if I meet 'em comin' back?"

Oakley smiled. "There'll still be some bonus gold in your poke. What I want now is an answer—from you or from them."

"When do you want me to light out?"

"On second thought, better get your grub now and ride out. I want you back here by sundown—with or without them. Bring them back belly down on their saddles if that's how you find them."

Buck Tanner reached the trail head well before midday. Dismounting, he walked to the rim and looked down. Nothing had happened to the dam. A half dozen men were still working on repairs. In the saddle again he rode around through the cover to see if Jake and Clayt had tethered their horses. There was no evidence beyond some recent droppings.

Not knowing what to expect, he decided to ride down the trail a bit. About two thirds of the way he stopped when several men working on the dam top discovered him and set aside their tools for their guns.

Cupping his mouth with his hands, Buck shouted at them. "Don't git jumpy! I'm Buck Tanner. I gotta see Clay."

When the men stood, still holding their weapons half ready, he continued. "I'm a friend. If Clayton's there tell him it's Buck Tanner—from the Gavilan. He'll know."

One of the men left the group and walked quickly to the nearby Adams house. In a moment, Buck saw Clayt come out walking with a marked limp. He waved and called again. Instantly, Clayt broke into a relieved grin. Motioning, he shouted, "Come on down, Buck. You're welcome. We've got some interesting company here—a man you know named Harmer!''

When Buck reached the bottom of the trail, half of the settlement was there, watching him curiously. Clayt was just finishing his fast introductions when Oss emerged from the Deyer house followed by Nelda and Kate. Buck hardly recognized the girl. He broke into a broad grin and ducked his head self-consciously. ''Well, I'm sure glad t'see the little lady's safe, too.'' Then, frowning as he swung down from the saddle, he indicated Clayt's leg. ''Looks like you got a bit stove up, son.''

Clayt put an arm around Buck's shoulder. ''It's nothing. I can guess what brings you here, friend. Oakley wants to know what happened to his two trusted hands.''

''That-there man's full up with nervous wonderin', Clay. He sure wants to know what's happened.'' He grinned, ''An' y'know, I'd sorta like to know myself.''

''Alright, Buck, let's put your horse in the corral and get over to the meeting house.'' He turned and pointed to a small, strongly built storage building near the barns. ''Jake's going to be spending some time with us, and after he talks, which he's surely going to do, he's going to be spending some time in a federal prison—if he lives to get there.''

The entire community gathered to listen as Clayt told Buck of the nearly messed up plot. The old man listened with wonderment and his head never stopped wagging. When Clayt finished, he ran a callused hand over the stubble on his cheek.

''After I found out what happened here, I come near believin' that the Good Lord was lookin' t'other way. Now I sure feel better—except that I wouldn't trust T.K. Oakley as far as I could throw a dead longhorn.''

Henry Deyer, who was sitting beside Clayt, leaned forward.

"You're going to have to ride back with a story for Oakley, aren't you?" Buck grinned and scratched the stubble on his cheek.

"Yes siree!" he replied, "and I'm sure lookin' forward. He told me to bring 'em belly down on their saddles if that was how I found 'em." Henry's smile was humorless.

"Well, my friend, you'll be riding back alone. But you can tell Oakley that you saw a couple of fresh graves up on top." He paused. "And tell him his horses are missing."

The old trail boss beamed with anticipation.

"...an I'm gonna hafta carry the sad news that ole Jake and young Clay here is probab'ly occupyin' same."

"For a minute," Clayt observed, "that was real close to the truth." Kate Williams's shoulders sagged and she lowered her head in an act of prayerful gratitude.

Rising, Clayt turned to his mother and Nelda. "Buck's got a hard ride and a hard time ahead of him. Let's send him on his way with a good noon dinner."

The meal was not hurried. After a bit of initial shyness at a properly set and served family meal, Buck answered questions easily about Oakley and Harmer without allowing his own growing hatred to color his responses. But it remained for Clayt to tell them of Buck Tanner's early life, of his dreams, his kindness at the hands of the Mormons, their slaughter, the mistaken death of his small son and later, his wife's death.

"I didn't really want to get into it," Buck said quietly, "on account of what you folks bin through." He brightened suddenly and patted his stomach. "But I sure as shoot..." He broke off with a sheepish expression and coughed. "But I sure wanta tell you folks that you've ruint me for Gavilan grub. Jes' plumb ruint me!"

Clayt and Henry rode with him to the top of the trail. In the piñon clump to the left, they walked him into the spot where they had found the bodies of the two gun slingers.

Buck stared at the stones outlining the graves.

"Lookin' back now," he said, "I reckon I never did trust them devils. That scrawny half-breed give me the willies. Never seen it before. He ach'lly slept with his eyes open."

"One thing," Clayt said, "you can truthfully tell Oakley that you didn't see any horses and you did see a couple of graves. He can put any bodies in them he cares to."

"He'll do more'n that," Buck agreed, "he'll also figger out that with you and Jake dead, he's not gonna be in any way to give you folks more trouble fur a long time—'least not until he can get a new crew together. And by that time, if you sweat a confession outa Jake—which ain't likely to happen until he's jes' before climbin' his last set of stairs— T.K.'s gonna be fresh outa any more hankerin' to blow things up!" He looked from one to the other. "I'll take off now, but I sure feel good about the way things is turnin' out. I got a notion if T.K. didn't think Jake was dead, he'd see to it himself!"

There were still two hours of working light when Buck turned his horse loose in the corral and pulled down some feed for the other animals there. Oakley sauntered over and stood watching him until he finished putting his things away. Buck was grateful that the superintendent had not begun the questioning immediately. When he was done Oakley indicated the wash trough.

"Clean up and come over to the house."

Still full from the first really fine meal he had eaten in years, Buck freshened up and found Oakley waiting for him on the porch.

Buck told him of finding two new graves. "I looked around up top but didn't see no horses."

"You'd have seen them if you'd been fool enough to go poking around their corral. Jake probably went off half cocked and got them killed for it." The only evidence of the man's deep hatred for the two who had bungled the job was the black diamond glint in his eyes and the taut muscles in his long, dark face.

When Buck finished his account, Oakley handed him a ten dollar gold piece, then turned abruptly without further talk and went inside. The old trail boss lingered uncertainly for a minute or so then left for the bunkhouse. The other hands glanced at him curiously from time to time, apparently waiting for him to speak. When he didn't they curbed their curiosity but the evidence was unsettling. Within a short time two riderless horses had been led in and now two more men were missing, one of them the foreman himself. The only conclusion possible was one that did not make for untroubled sleep.

Chapter Twelve

Oss rode into Las Vegas with orders from his father to find out if the new Federal Marshall had arrived. Once again his source of information was the garrulous old fellow who met the stages and guarded the express shipments.

"He ain't showed up yet, mister. All we got is still that fool town constable who oughta be in the calaboose hisself fur stealin' his fifty a month!"

Oss thanked him, watered his horse, and turned back down the rutted wagon road leading south. The news he brought was disappointing.

"Did he give you any idea when a new man would be there?" Henry asked.

"No, father," Oss replied. "I asked him and he took ten minutes to tell me that he didn't know and that the stage driver from Santa Fe didn't know either. He also said Vegas was getting to be a rough town and the constable—or sheriff or whatever he is—is always away or looking the other way when anything happens. I don't think we're going to get much help." The reaction to the discouraging news could be clearly read in the faces of the survivors. Jakob Gruen spoke for most of them.

"If we've got to wait, then there's no use to put up with him banging and kicking and spouting filth. Break the man down, Henry, like you said you used to do with prisoners. Get the murdering devil to say he did it. Clayt knows. Tanner knows the same—that he did it—or maybe did it for that Oakley fella.''

When a majority of settlers expressed their agreement, Henry decided to bear down harder. In the room, with Clayt and Oss standing guard, he began the interrogaton that, as an officer, he had used to wring confessions out of Northern spies. Once identified, they were executed summarily. In Harmer's case, there was more than enough justification to hang him immediately, except for the promise to Asa.

The door to the storage shed had been left open to vent some of the stifling heat. Even so, sweat trickled down the necks of the four of them as Henry battered Jake Harmer with Gatling-gun rapidity, alternating the same questions in an effort to confuse and trick the man into admissions.

Jake Harmer proved tougher than expected. He alternately sneered and laughed at them, and not once did he back off an inch. Instead, he countered with a tirade of vile abuse and threats of his own, their certain fate when Oakley and the new men he was hiring blew them to Hell with dynamite sticks raining down on them from the canyon rim. The foreman's language was so foul that Clayt picked up the half full slop bucket in which Harmer relieved himself. ''Shut up, Harmer, or you're going to get this filth right in the face!''

''Go ahead,'' Harmer sneered. ''It'll be one more thing to even up fur, you rotten double crossin' son of...'' A sudden pained grunt cut off the last word as Oss gave Harmer a vicious jab in the solar plexus with the barrel of his ten-gauge shotgun.

''As God is my witness, I'd love to splatter your guts all over that wall behind you, but the law's going to take care of you, Harmer, unless one of us gets fed up and saves them the trouble!''

Jake Harmer sank back on his bunk trying to recover the

wind that had been knocked out of him. Henry stared at him with utter disgust, then motioned to Clayt and Oss.

"Let's let him stew in his own juice for a while longer."

Speechless with rage, Jake Harmer slumped on his bunk. More like a trapped animal than a human, his eyes darted to every corner of his improvised jail cell, searching for anything he could use for a weapon. As he pushed himself upright, his hand moved the sideboard that held his blankets and straw ticking in place. Trying it, he found it could be torn loose by hand. Carefully, to keep the old square nails from squeaking, he pulled the narrow plank free. From both ends three-inch-long rusty, hand-forged nails protruded, long enough to penetrate the skull of an unwary victim.

A vicious smile spread across his face as hope flared. If he could surprise Clayton and get his gun, he might be able to shoot his way out. Carefully he pried the nails straight at one end and flattened them at the other.

The angle of the shadows he could see from the high, foot-square barred window at the back of the building told him that he'd have to wait at least an hour before they came with his food.

He passed the time planning his strategy. In the end he decided not to be caught holding the club. As his eyes darted around the cell-like room, they fell on the half full slop bucket. Suddenly he laughed. "He was gonna throw this in my face, was he?" He pulled the container of filth over to the foot of his bunk, then took the bludgeon and stood it beside the door frame. Shock and surprise were his only chance. If he could catch Clayton off guard, slosh him full in the face with his filth, grab the club and drive it into his head, and snatch his revolver, all in a matter of seconds, he could shoot them both, make a break for it, and head downstream. There were a dozen places where he could hide until dark. Then he would scramble out of the canyon, make his way to Tres Dedos and get a horse from Santos. He'd run it flat out to the Gavilan and get it to Oakley. It would be alright from then on. The superintendent would be as eager as he to square accounts.

Harmer's jaws clamped in deadly determination. He'd do it! He'd make it, and when he did, it would be the end of those water-thieving settlers, and the beginning of a new place for him because he had figured out now, how to get rid of the settlers once and for all. The hand bombs he'd improvised, and the new explosive, dynamite, would do the trick. All hell would rain down on them from the canyon rim and they couldn't do a thing about it but what they ought to do—die in their own tracks.

Confident that he could get away with it, Harmer waited with nervous anticipation. As the time grew nearer he went over each move in his mind until it was letter perfect. Shock would be added to surprise and even Clayton, fast as he was, couldn't do a thing about it.

When he heard the hammering on the dam repairs stop he climbed up on the bunk in time to see Clayt coming with a covered tin plate of food. Walking behind him came Oss carrying his ten-gauge double-barreled shotgun.

Controlling his excitement, he turned his back to the door and stood facing the bucket. When he heard the lock and chain hang free, he prepared to use the bucket.

"Your grub's here, Harmer," Clayt called. "Sit down on the bunk."

"Come in," Harmer replied. "I'm usin' the bucket."

Oss pushed the door open a few inches and peered in.

"That's what he's doing alright," he said.

"Go ahead, open it," Clayt ordered. The rusty iron hinges squeaked as the door scraped free of the sill. Clayt started to enter. He had just cleared the doorway, with Oss close behind him, when Harmer suddenly reached down, grabbed the bucket, whirled, and threw the contents full in his face.

Clayt let out a shocked roar of disgust, dropped the food

and lifted both hands to his face. Catlike, Harmer leaped at him and snatched the Smith and Wesson from its holster. His hand was sweaty and the gun butt was wet. In his anxiety to pull back the hammer he lost his hold and the gun dropped to the floor. Panicked for a split second, he recovered, grabbed the spiked plank and raised it to strike. Oss let out a warning cry. Instinctively, he slammed his body against Clayt's. The bludgeon grazed Clayt's ear, struck his shoulder, and broke into two pieces. The lethal nails in the free end fell harmlessly to the floor. Clayt let out a bellow of rage and charged Harmer. The force sent them sprawling backwards on the bunk with Clayt on top. Diving for it, Oss recovered the revolver, wiped the butt on his pants and shoved it into Clayt's hand.

"You don't need excuses now," he shouted. "Kill him and get it over with!"

Clayt pushed the gun aside with his left arm and fended off an attempt by Harmer to claw out his eyes. "Yeah! Let's git it over with," Harmer screamed. "Let's finish it!"

As he uttered the challenge he heaved upright and toppled Clayt off the bunk. As Clayt recovered his feet, Harmer lunged with arms wide and grasped him around the waist in a rough and tumble bear hug. In the past his viselike grip had broken the ribs and squeezed the wind out of many an adversary. Clayt drove a knee into his groin and broke the grip long enough to free an arm. Harmer tripped him and they both went down into the sheet of slime smeared over most of the floor.

Oss, unable to use his shotgun in such close quarters, grasped it by the barrel and prepared to use it as a club. Twice he lifted it to strike but could not get a clean blow at Harmer whose sweat-soaked face was jammed against Clayt's chest. Catching sight of him out of the corner of his eye, Clayt warned, "Don't try it! I want to finish it my way!"

For a moment Oss backed off and considered running for

help, but he didn't dare leave in case the bull-strong foreman managed to gain a critical advantage.

Again, Harmer clawed viciously at Clayt's eyes and a horny thumbnail broke the flesh on his cheekbone. When the blood began to cloud his vision, Clayt smeared it away on the foreman's head, and managed to jerk an arm free. Making a fist, he hammered short punches against Harmer's cheek until he twisted violently, broke free, and scrambled to his feet.

"We'll finish it *my* way," Harmer gasped, "*my* way!" As he repeated the words he charged full against Clayt and both of them went staggering toward the wall. A half step before Clayt's head would have smashed against one of the rough uprights that supported the rafters, he twisted. Harmer took the full impact on the back of his head. Hurt and momentarily dazed, he stared at Clayt with his arms loose and useless. Instantly, Clayt shot a deadly left fist at Harmer's face and an iron hard right hammered the foreman's cheekbone. Then, in a split second, the right smashed into the man's sore belly. He let out a grunt and pitched forward. As he did Clayt battered him with a wild, unmerciful flurry of blows until Harmer toppled unconscious.

Clayt stood over him for a few seconds, then he recovered the pieces of the broken bludgeon and the bucket.

"Let's get out of here," he gasped.

Oss set the chain and padlock on the door and nodded toward the houses. "Nelda and Kate are coming looking."

"I don't want them to see me like this. Tell Nelda to bring me some fresh clothes and leave them on the bank. I'm going down to the pool below the dam and clean up." He gave Oss a critical examination. "And you'd better ask her to bring some for you, too. Right now, we're both pretty high."

Clayt didn't see the horrified expressions on the girls' faces as Oss, standing some feet apart from them, explained what had happened.

Both Clayt and Oss were bathing naked in the cold pool when Henry appeared carrying their fresh clothing. "The girls told me what happened," he said. "Now I've really got plans for that foul-hearted Hellhound! Before I'm through with him, he's going to wish to God that you had killed him."

Chapter Thirteen

Harmer, forced to live in the mess of his own making, was put on one skimpy meal a day and just enough water to keep him alive. Henry, with both Clayt and Oss standing guard, and with two other armed men outside as a precaution, pounded away on the prisoner until he was brought to the ragged edge of collapse. Finally, after nearly a week of torment, treatment that brought appeals for at least some mercy from several of the women, under heavy guard, Harmer was taken below the dam to the pool and made to wash. He was given fresh clothes, "A dead man's clothes," Henry reminded him as they chained him to a tree until two of the women who volunteered to do it, scrubbed the little storage house.

Reluctantly, Henry put Harmer back on two meals. Standing with Clayt and Oss as he was returned to his prison, the older man spoke to him quietly.

"We're going to break you, Harmer. Marshall or no marshall, you're going to roast in here until you tell us who put you up to it. It's up to you. If you can prove that you were obeying orders, that somebody above you put you up to it, it could go easier with you. You might get off with life."

"I'll see ya in hell before I tell ya anything!" he growled. "Go on. Do yer damnedest!"

Henry moistened his lips and nodded. "Alright, Harmer. We'll take you at your word. I'll make you a promise. A week from today you'll be begging us to hand you over to the law." He started to turn away. Pointedly, he added, "And by that time, it may be too late for you."

Within two days the cramped little strong house was a sweat box again. Dressed only in trousers, Harmer waited and wondered. They wouldn't kill him. He was certain of that. For some reason they were dead set on letting the law do that. Once T.K. knew what was happening to him, the favors the law granted to cattlemen and railroads would get him off. If he had to wait that long to get even, it would be worth it. Hatred for the settlers burned in him like bile. His hatred for Clayton was beyond measure. He would kill him an inch at a time. Lost in grim revelry, he recalled the story a Comanche chief told: "More cuts than bird has feathers— man no dead yet!"

He climbed up on the foot of the bunk and pressed his face against the bars. By sundown, the canyon had cooled a bit and the fresh air revived him some.

As twilight faded the settlers began to appear carrying lanterns. They were heading for the meeting house. Many of them seemed to pause to look in his direction. It was clear to Harmer that the assembly had something to do with him. He guessed they would be discussing more ways to wear him down, to make him talk. Well, they could burn in hell and he'd live long enough to light the fire!

Standing by the lectern, Henry Deyer waited for the people to take their places on the log benches. He had called the meeting. It was one he did not want just now, but he felt the changing mood of many of the surviving settlers demanded an air clearing. When the last of them had settled themselves, Jakob Gruen rose and indicated those sitting beside and behind him on the rear benches.

121

"Henry," he began, "in order to keep this matter from running on late, I've been asked to say how they feel, including my own feelings about Harmer."

Henry nodded. "Please go on, Jakob. State the case."

"Well, make no mistake, we all want to see the man convicted under law and killed under law. That's how Asa wanted it and we do, too. But if Asa was still with us, we wonder if he wouldn't have had a bellyful of the man's filthy mouth by now."

"He probably would have, Jakob, but none of us could know that the marshall was shot by rustlers trying to perform his duty, and that another one would take so long replacing him. I think he would still have argued for patience."

Jakob turned to Mary Adams who was seated beside Clayt and Oss. Nelda and Kate sat with him.

"You knew him best of all, Mary. Do you think his patience would stretch this far?"

Mary frowned and pursed her lips thoughtfully.

"I believe so," she said. "Asa always kept promises, and he expected others' promises to be kept."

Gruen toyed with the wooden peg fastener on his homespun blouse. Turning, he addressed the same question to Clayt.

"Father had patience enough to put this settlement together. He would have had patience enough to do the necessary to keep it together."

Henry Deyer, standing with his work-hardened hands braced on the edge of the lectern, nodded in agreement.

Jakob did not expect support for precipitous action from the Adams family, but they were the minority. With the vision of his wife dead in his arms, he was no longer a part of the minority urging restraint. He wanted retribution soon—tonight if possible. He didn't care to be reminded still again that if they took the law into their own hands, there would be no end to their troubles and, inevitably, it would mean the end of Red Creek as soon as Oakley and whoever he answered to could execute another attack.

"So, Henry," Jakob continued, "there's some differences here and we have always settled those by a vote with the majority's wish being respected."

Henry Deyer straighted and regarded the people he had been instrumental in recruiting to form the settlement. Under his unblinking scrutiny they grew uncomfortable.

"So, *Jakob*," he said, deliberately, "am I to understand that you all want to bring this situation to a head and vote on it tonight?"

"We do, Henry."

"And what we'll be voting on is the immediate hanging of Jake Harmer, his being punished by order of a kangaroo court?"

The German silversmith shook his head. "We are not a mob, a kangaroo court, Henry. We don't want to railroad the man. He's guilty by his own mouth." He turned to Clayt. "The man as much as confessed to Clayt. So did Oakley. And Tanner will bear witness too—before God. No injustice will be done here, Henry...." A murmur of agreement ran through the hall.

"We've had weeks of the man's rotten-hearted language and threats. He tried to kill Clayt and Oss. He would have killed any of us who got in his way if he'd blasted his way free—" He spread his arms in supplication. "Do we need any more cause? We pray to a just God. It is written, 'Eye for eye, tooth for tooth, hand for hand, foot for foot.'"

Henry Deyer, who conducted the sabbath services, lowered his head. A thin smile softened his stern face. The words had first been written by Hammurabi, two thousand years before Christ.

"It is also written, Jakob, my friend, from the lips of our Savior, that we 'resist not evil: but whosoever shall smite thee on thy right cheek, turn to him the other also....'"

123

As he spoke the words from the Sermon on the Mount, Henry recalled how long he had struggled to determine their true meaning—that nothing was said of cowardice, that peace could be won only by having the courage to turn from violence and by dedicating a life to the observance of God's Laws.

Here and there in the hall, he could hear some whispered grumbling, dissent over the apparent contradictions in the Scriptures. He understood it well. Wagging a finger at Jakob Gruen, he continued, "'An eye for an eye, a tooth for a tooth is the law of battle: a sword for a sword, a bullet for a bullet, a life for a life—and never will there be a real victor.'' He shook his head sadly. "How well Asa and I—and thousands of our comrades in arms—learned that."

Jakob raised a fist and shook it. "Is it God's Law that we should turn the other cheek to that mad man locked up over there, that we should turn him over to man's law, probably to be set free?'' The words came in a near shout.

Henry Deyer, who so recently and so tragically had become the reluctant patriarch of the settlement, lifted both hands in a staying gesture.

"Some things are beyond my wisdom, Jakob, but I understand as deeply as any of you, the pain in your hearts. What I am asking for is the courage to honor a promise to a man, which I also take to be a law blessed by God."

Jakob remained silent with his fist still clenched. After a moment, he lowered it and turned questioning eyes to the others.

Clayt rose slowly. "But for the grace of God, I'd be lying in the newest grave across the creek. You know how I'll vote. You know how Henry and Oss will vote, how my family will vote." He rested a hand on his mother's shoulder. "I have not asked to speak...."

"Speak up," Henry said. "Speak up."

"I have not asked to speak because I know the outcome

of your vote. The outcome will be judgment by our law and I'm bound by it.'' He turned to face the others. ''I know what Henry can do to get the confession, the kind we need to get Harmer to the law. I also know that, confession or not, there is a chance that he will not be convicted, especially if it comes to word against word, his against ours. If we judge him guilty and execute him ourselves, Oakley will hire another Harmer to do his dirty work and we won't know a peaceful hour for the rest of our lives here. In this country—and it's starting now—power is measured by the size of the herds going to the railroad. That is another law—not written down—but a law just the same.'' He turned back to the lectern. ''I'm asking this for you, Henry—and for all of us—do you think you can wring a confession on paper out of Jake Harmer?''

''As God is my witness, Clayt, I will! I'll get one, and it will be legally witnessed in Las Vegas. I just need some more time.''

Turning back to the others, Clayt said, ''To honor another promise, will you give Henry the time...?''

''And the help,'' Henry interjected.

''The time *and* the help,'' Clayt repeated, ''to get the job done?''

There was a moment of hesitation, then a murmur of agreement started, punctuated by a somewhat reluctant showing of hands.

The meeting ran for another hour as Henry Deyer outlined his plan.

''The reason I know this will work,'' he explained, ''is because we found that nothing tears a prisoner down faster than holding out hope for his life, then snatching it away. Usually you don't have to do it more than once. This Harmer fellow is tough, but I think I see signs of cracking. I'm not only going to need your help but your patience, too.'' Indicating Nelda, he said, ''And you're going to have to play the hardest part, one you're not going to like at all, but it's got to be done. There's no way Harmer can get out of that storage shed without help, and you're going to have to pretend to give it to him, Nelda, because some of the women have had enough.''

When he had finished a detailed explanation of how the plan was to work, Kate turned to Nelda and whispered, ''Do you think you can do it?'' Nelda drew in a deep breath and nodded.

''I'll do it. How good, I don't know. But I'll try.''

''If you don't want to,'' Kate said, ''if Clayt will let me, I'll do it.''

Nelda hugged her. ''You've been through enough, Kate. It's my place and I'll do it.''

Chapter Fourteen

Shortly before noon the following day, Buck Tanner re-appeared.

"I cain't stay. I gotta make up time. But two things ya oughta know. Them new owners is comin' in fur a meetin' with Oakley: They'll be on tomorra's stage. I'm ridin' in now with a poke full of sweet money to begin hirin' new hands. Oakley's hotter than a stirred up hornet. He wants me to git at least six new hands, tough ones, he says, who knows cows and guns equal—and who likes money better than whiskey."

Clayt managed a grin. "You may be in town for a while!"

Tanner gave Clayt and Henry a knowing smile. "I plan on havin' me quite a time fillin' that order. They ain't many's gonna do."

He swung into the saddle with the ease of a younger man.

"I got one more thing. Y'oughta git this law business settled real soon. T.K.'s so mad at ya both gittin' kilt that he's even bein' nice to me!" He reined his horse toward the dam and added, "He figgers with you two dead and buried, he's in the clear. He's gittin' set to worry you folks a lot more."

The men who had gathered around Henry and Clayt watched until Buck Tanner reached the rim and waved. Then they went back to the meeting house to complete the plans that would begin late in the afternoon.

An hour before sundown angry voices, men's and women's, brought Harmer off the bunk to peer from the little window. A group of settlers, apparently wrangling among themselves, were getting things off their chests a few yards away.

Oss was carrying a hangman's noose at the end of a coil of heavy halter rope. When Nelda tried to restrain him, he pulled away. "I don't care about waiting for the law." He pointed to the strong house. "That mad dog in there tried to drive a spike club into our heads and shoot his way out." Pointing toward the trail, he continued in an agitated voice, "There's no marshall in Vegas, and God only knows when there will be one. We're not waiting. If you don't want to watch a killer die, then go back to your houses."

Harmer saw Clayton pushing his way into the angry gathering. When he took his sister's arm she jerked it away.

"I don't care! You made a promise to father and you're just as low as that man if you break it."

Clayt took her by the shoulders. "You were there when we voted. That is our law and the majority voted to hang the man in the morning."

A sudden cry of agreement went up from the dozen or so gathered. It seemed to Harmer that the girl and only three or four others were for waiting until he could be taken to the law. In the midst of the argument, Henry Deyer appeared.

"Alright now. I don't want to take the law into my hands either, but we have no choice. Our law says we act by majority. You've had your say. In the morning we'll do the necessary. Get on back to fixing your suppers. It'll be over with and he'll be buried up top with his cronies by sunrise."

Harmer watched the crowd disperse. The girl was still arguing with Clayton and Oss as they walked away. She was obviously very upset by the decision. He was about to leave the window when he saw the older man take the hanging rope from Oss.

Moving deliberately, he examined the noose and measured off several arm spans of rope as they walked to an old sycamore about twenty yards away. They stopped beneath a stout limb some ten to twelve feet above the ground. Deyer studied it briefly then tossed the free end over it and secured it to a smaller limb lower down.

Anxiety ran to the edge of fear as Harmer watched Clayt test the noose then slip it around his neck. Holding with both hands to keep it from choking him, he signaled them to pull. When his feet hit the ground he motioned for them to pull it higher. Jerking and writhing, he struggled to touch, then signaled his approval. On the ground again, they freed him and secured the rope in place.

As he watched with morbid fascination, Harmer saw two men approaching pulling a heavy hand cart. On it was a newly nailed together, rough box coffin. Suddenly he caught a vision of himself, hands and feet trussed, swinging by the neck until he was blue in the face, his tongue protruding, dripping saliva, and his body contorting in death throes. The older man's words came back now, whispering through his mind. They were not a threat, just a cold, quiet promise: "Alright, Harmer, we'll take you at your word. I'll make you a promise. A week from today you'll be begging us to hand you over to the law."

Again, as he stared at the dangling rope, already measured to his neck, and the ample coffin ready to receive his stinking body, Harmer felt a change, felt himself slip from anxiety and the bravado of hollow threats to the first real fear he had known.

Grasping the bars, he jammed his face against them and screamed, "Alright! I'll tell ya what really happened! The God's honest truth! I'll tell ya who done it, who put me up to it. I swear to God it's the truth. It weren't my doin'!"

Clayt turned when he heard him. He listened for a moment then walked a few yards closer.

"You want the God's honest truth, Jake? I'll tell it to you. We know what happened. We know what Oakley told you to do and why, and we know why you did it!" He paused briefly. Then, in a chilling, matter of fact, voice, he added, "Tomorrow morning, Jake, you can tell the God's honest truth to the devil!"

When Clayt rejoined the others and they started to leave, Harmer remained silent. For a time he clung to the bars, then let them slip from his hands as he crumpled on the bunk.

Clayt and Oss found him lying helpless, face down when they brought the food. He made no sign that he heard them enter and leave. He was lost in a hell, mostly of his own making, not caring now what happened.

When he finally stirred and found the food it was cold and he had no stomach for it. Standing on the foot of the bunk, he peered through the window again. Even in the moonless night he could make out the ragged silhouette of the old sycamore tree and the limb with the rope hanging from it. Several yards away he could see the darker shape of the work cart and the coffin. In the distance a lantern bobbed along, carried by someone on an after-dark errand.

It caused an eerie feeling, for it reminded him of those other lanterns swinging crazily as they were carried out of their homes by panicked settlers minutes after he and his two gunslingers had blown the dam. He remembered what easy targets they had made, and the trails of flame as they were thrown into the pond or dashed to the ground by those who fell with them to scream for help...or to die.

He remembered other screams, those of innocent women and children, murdered in cold blood when he had ridden through Lawrence, Kansas, with Quantrill and his raiders eight years earlier. Somehow he had managed to block out the vision, if not the memory of them. But now, unaccountably, he could hear them again harking back through the years—and even clearer, through the last weeks since he, with perverted glee, had followed Oakley's order to the letter... and then some.

As he stood, still older memories assailed him, going back to his childhood in West Virginia, the pain of punishment and the fear of more, that he had blocked out since his tenth year, when his drunken father had beaten him near to death for stealing a gallon jug of raw White Mule and selling it to a hunter for five cents and a rusty, bone-handled skinning knife with a broken point. But this was a new fear. It parched his mouth, blurred his eyes, and knotted his guts. After he had put that first terror behind him he swore he would never know fear again. And he proved it to himself and to those he rode with during the war—always up at the head of the column, just behind Bloody Bill Anderson, who tied scalps to his bridle reins, and Bill Todd, whose rage fed on blood.

For a time he paced the ten-foot-square room like a caged animal. It was easy to tell yourself you weren't afraid to die when you were sure you never would. You didn't say it. You just proved it. You proved it most when you risked it most.

Punching a fist into his palm, he said, half aloud, "By God, I'll prove it again! When they come fur me in the mornin', I'll prove it again. I'll kill at least one of 'em with my bare hands, but I swear to God they'll never hang me to die slow. They'll have to shoot me first. If I'm gonna go, that's how I'm gonna go. Not like some yella-bellied horse thief!"

Harmer did not know how long he'd been trying to stifle his fear with rage when suddenly something struck one of the iron grill bars in the little window and fell to the floor at his feet.

Startled, he picked it up and discovered that someone had thrown a smooth pebble through the window. Cautiously, he climbed up on the foot of the bunk and peered out. Suspecting some sort of trap, he remained silent. Then, as he was about to leave the window, he heard a female voice calling his name softly. The voice called several times more before he decided to answer.

"Who is it? What d'ya want?" he answered in a hoarse whisper.

"Never mind. Just listen to me, Harmer. They're going to hang you in the morning. They're not going to wait for the law." There was a pause. "Do you hear me?"

"I hear ya."

"Some of us have had enough. We want you out of here. You can't go back to the Gavilan. Oakley's going to put all of the blame on you. He thinks you're dead. If you try to go back he'll kill you for sure, to keep your mouth shut."

Suddenly he realized that if he could not go back to the Gavilan there would be no way he could square up with the Red Creekers. He had counted on T.K.'s anger to finish the job. Desperate now, he pressed his face to the bars.

"I swear to God, I told ya the truth. It was Oakley's idea. He figgered the whole thing out."

"It doesn't make any difference now," the voice replied. "You've admitted that you did it and so has he. We know that. But we want you out of Red Creek, now—tonight. If you're smart, you'll get out of the territory. It's the only chance you've got!"

"I can't go anywheres 'til I git out of this stinkin' box," he replied.

"I know that, Harmer. Now listen—I've got a pinch bar here. I'm going to push it through to you. Pry up a couple of floor planks. There's room under there for you to crawl. Crawl to the right, away from the houses, then head for the big willow clump downstream past the last house. There's a horse waiting for you there. Cross the creek down there, then ride back up the other side to the trail. Do it right or you're dead, Harmer. We know Oakley put you up to it. The law will take care of him when the time comes. We just want you out of here. We don't want any more taking of life. Do you understand?''

"Gimme the bar!'' Harmer whispered eagerly. "I'll go! You'll never see me agin!''

A moment later the pinch bar scraped against the metal grill. He snatched it, jumped down, dropped to the floor, and ran his hands over the planks.

Unable to believe that it was happening, he forced the flattened end between two of the lengths of rough flooring and began prying. As he put more pressure on the pinch bar the old plank began to bow and crack.

On the side of the house where they could not be seen, Clayt waited with a lantern. Oss had a hammer. Both were kneeling beside the open crawl space.

Nelda joined them. "He's got it,'' she whispered.

Clayt gave her neck an affectionate squeeze. "You did a fine job.''

"I hated it!'' she replied. "Anything to do with that man makes me feel dirty!''

Oss touched her arm. "When we get through with him, you're going to feel as clean as a hound's tooth. We all are.''

"You've still got Oakley.''

"Sure we have,'' Clayt answered, "but when he finds out we've got his dead foreman very much alive, we're not going to have much trouble with him for a long time.''

"That's more hope than we'd have with Harmer on the loose. It's a chance we've got to take, I guess,'' Nelda replied.

The exchange was interrupted by the loud squeaking of rusty old handmade square nails pulling away.

Harmer broke off prying, afraid to breathe. When he heard nothing outside, he went to work again. In spite of his caution, the old nails groaned as they began to move.

It took him ten minutes to get the first plank loosened enough to move it to the side. The second one would be easier. He'd have an edge to pry against. Trying to be as quiet as possible, he wedged the flattened end of the bar beneath the edge of the second plank and the floor joist. It would not go easily. Using his hand for a maul he pounded against the notched nail's pulling end and managed to get a little leverage. When he applied downward pressure on it the first nail came loose with a dry screech.

Harmer cursed under his breath and held the bar in place, not daring to move it. Just as he was about to continue, he heard footsteps outside. Freezing, he listened and a cold sweat broke out on his face when he realized that someone was coming to the door.

"Harmer! What's going on in there?" It was Clayton! "You having a restless last night on earth?"

Terrified, Harmer dropped the pinch bar through the opening and reset the plank. Frantically, he tried to fit the nails back into their original holes. Bent in the prying, they wouldn't go. When he heard the padlock open and the chain hang free, he had no recourse but to stand on the planks to try to bend them flat.

When Clayt entered with the lantern in one hand and his six-shooter in the other, Oss was right behind him, carrying a hammer.

For a moment, Clayt held the lantern high, looking around.

"Go sit down, Harmer. We were on our way to fix up a little something for your going away in the morning and we thought we heard some nails pulling loose. Don't usually hear that around here after quitting time."

Lowering the lantern to inspect the floor, he pretended surprise to find a loose plank. "Good thing we came by," he said. "If you'd kept your eyes open, you might have found this one and missed your necktie party."

Oss kneeled down and spiked the plank back in place.

As he got up, he turned to Harmer. "Unless you've got real good fingernails we'll expect to find you here just before sunup. We thought about hanging you by lantern light tonight to save a breakfast, but it seemed like a waste of good oil.'

For one fleeting moment, Harmer braced his muscles for a suicide attack. Clayt smiled. "Don't try it, Jake. We want a good turnout for your last trip!"

When they had gone and the lock had been reset, Harmer sank on the bunk, sick with disappointment. The pressure of frustration and unscreamed threats filled his eyes with tears. Sitting hunched over, he jammed his fists viciously into his middle to keep from sobbing. There was no chance to loosen the planks again. His fingers moved involuntarily to his throat. The hangman's knot would come up behind his left ear. They'd stand him on the cart—probably on top of his own coffin to get a longer drop—then jerk it from under him. He'd drop no more than six feet—not enough to break his neck—and they'd stand there enjoying their hatred of him as he slowly strangled doing the Mexican rope dance.

He jumped up, shaking his fists over his head. "Oh, God!" he moaned, "gimme one more chance at 'em. Just one more chance!"

The stream of half sobbed curses that followed was interrupted by another pebble. Harmer jumped up on the bunk and jammed his face against the bars.

"Are you down there?" he gasped.

"I'm here," the voice answered. "It's all clear. You can go now. Hurry up!"

"I can't!" he cried in a broken voice. "They almost caught me. I had to drop the bar under the floor!"

For several minutes there was silence, then he heard the voice again. "I've got it. Take it!"

He grabbed the tool and with near recklessness, he pried both planks loose and lowered himself to the ground under the house. It was pitch black.

For a long moment he stayed dead still getting his wind. Then he began to crawl to his right as the voice had instructed.

In the clear, staying low, he scurried along the creek bank. He passed two houses. Both were dark. Beyond them was another house. A light shone in the window. Undecided, he stayed stock still, crouched below the bank. Just as he was about to continue, he heard a door open. A moment later Jakob Gruen emerged carrying a lantern. Harmer watched as he moved to the outhouse. It was part of the plan to add to Harmer's frustration. Jakob left the door open, lingered briefly, then returned to the house. Instead of reentering, he carried the lantern around, deliberately pretending to be looking for something.

For Harmer it was an eternity. When the man finally returned to the house, he got up. Abandoning caution, he all but ran to the dark stand of willows.

Pushing through them, he found the promised horse tethered there already saddled. With a stifled cry of relief, he undid the halter, gathered the reins, and mounted.

Again, he would have to use restraint until he could get to the trail. The creek in front of the willows was shallow and wide. Fording it would be no trouble if the animal didn't stumble. Tightening the reins a bit, he dug his heels into its sides. The horse tried to move but behaved strangely. Harmer kicked him. The animal tried to rear and nearly fell. Cursing it aloud now, he kicked even harder. This time the animal let out a short whinny of protest as its legs buckled and collapsed onto its front knees.

Harmer leaped from the saddle, grabbed the bit ring and tried to pull the horse back to its feet. The animal reared its head and tried to paw itself upright. It was then that Harmer realized that it was hobbled.

Frantically, he loosened the hobble and remounted. This time the animal reared and fell. Screaming curses, Harmer saw that its rear legs had been chained around the base of the willows and padlocked.

Suddenly, beyond control now that he realized how well

he had been tricked, he charged out of the cover. Screaming curses, he plunged into the waist-deep current. Behind him lanterns appeared. Turning, he screamed, "Come an' git me, ya dirty rotten, double-crossin' skunks! Come an' git me an' git it over with!"

There was no answer behind him. Suddenly, in front of him as he struggled to reach the far bank, lanterns flared and he saw six men armed with shotguns and rifles waiting for him. In the forefront stood Clayt and Oss with Henry Deyer.

Letting out an insane scream that echoed down the canyon, Harmer suddenly collapsed at the water's edge. As the current began moving his legs downstream, Clayt and Oss waded in and dragged him onto the shore.

Minutes later, bound hand and foot, Harmer was returned to the strong room. The last of his will crushed, he broke down sobbing, then rolled over and buried his face in the sweat-fouled blanket.

Chapter Fifteen

It was still dark when Harmer heard the padlock being opened. An endless nightmare, as frightening during his restless wakeful hours as it was during his intermittent sleep, had reduced him to an unreasoning wreck.

Beyond caring, he waited.

Armed, Clayt entered the room, followed by Oss and his father, both carrying shotguns. Setting the lantern down he said, "Alright, Harmer, it's time to go."

When there was no response, Clayt repeated the words. When there was still no reply, he nodded to Oss. While Henry Deyer stood guard, they bound Harmer's arms to his torso with the fettering rope that Oss carried, rolled him face down on the bunk, and bound his hands behind him. Using a longer length of rope, they took several turns around his waist and pulled him upright.

"Get on your feet, Harmer!" Clayt ordered.

Again, there was no response.

"Get up on your feet!" Clayt snapped.

After a long moment, with Oss's help he pulled Harmer erect and forced him stumbling, through the door. As they rounded the side of the house toward the hanging tree, Harmer saw a large group of settlers there. Lit by their lanterns, they made an eerie assemblage. Dimly, he understood they were waiting to watch him die.

When they were close enough for him to see, he discovered the work cart and coffin were gone. In their place were four saddled horses.

Clayt grasped his shoulder and shook him.

"We've had a change of plans, Harmer. The four of us are going for a little ride." He steered the foreman toward a horse wearing only a saddle, a halter, and a long lead.

Holding him on each side by the shoulders, Clayt and Oss boosted him high enough for two men from the gathering to get a boot in a stirrup, then they forced his leg over the cantle. The men then shoved his right boot into the stirrup and lashed it there. When Clayt finished with the left foot, he threaded a length of lariat through the bonds that bound Harmer's upper arms to his side, then brought the free ends around his body and around the cantle, securely fastening him into the saddle. One turn was then taken around Harmer's slumping upper body to hold him in an upright position.

Satisfied that all was in order, Clayt and the two Deyers mounted. Oss rode beside Clayt holding the halter lead on Harmer's mount. His father brought up the rear. When he was in place he repeated a command he had given so many times in the past, "Alright men, move out!"

As they started for the dam top and the trail at the far side of the creek, not a word was spoken by the spectators who, filled with cold hatred, watched until the Gavilan foreman and his captors disappeared in the darkness.

The ride to Las Vegas went slowly at first, but with a blood-red sunrise lightening as they rode and the first long, slanting rays of the new day tinting the Sangre de Cristo range off to the northwest, the pace quickened. Conversation had been sporadic and none of it touched on their plans.

Harmer, relieved that he was apparently being given a temporary reprieve, grunted complaints about the tightness of his bonds and occasional veiled, half-hearted threats. All were ignored.

The constable, whose absenteeism was a common cause for complaint, was found in his cubbyhole of an office shortly after eight o'clock.

Clayt, who had inquired and was told the man's name was Boyd Jones, introduced himself and explained their business.

"The marshall shoulda bin here two weeks ago," the constable replied. "Any business you got is territory business. I don't have no authority, except on town matters."

"Are you saying that nobody knows when a new marshall will be here?" Clayt asked.

"That's what I'm sayin', and I'm also sayin' real clear, that I won't give your prisoner the time of day...and you folks neither."

Clayt thought for a moment. "Alright. We understand that."

Henry moved up beside Clayt. "Look, mister, we don't want you to do a damned thing you shouldn't do. All we want is a responsible officer of the law to witness this man's confession of murder. You're an officer of the law, aren't you?"

"I'm constable, mister. I guess that says it."

"Fine," Henry replied, "then there's no reason why you can't legally witness a confession of murder I have here when the prisoner signs it."

Suddenly revived, Harmer shouted, "I ain't signin' nuthin' these rotten, double-crossin' water thieves has writ down! Nuthin'!"

Ignoring him, Clayt dismounted and walked up to the constable who had been nervously polishing his badge on the underside of his sleeve.

"This man has confessed to us—and so has his boss—that he was ordered to kill our people and blow up our dam down on Red Creek."

The constable's narrow brow wrinkled into a frown and his heavy jowls shook jellylike as he pretended to think, "Never heard of the place."

"That's because we mind our own business," Clayt replied. "But you're going to hear about us now because we'll never quit until we see this murdering madman brought to justice and hanged." He moved a half step closer and the town constable backed off.

Thrusting his face closer, Clayt said, "Mister, I demand that you do your duty and witness this man's confession. That's all we want from you. We'll do the rest of our business with the territorial marshall whenever he shows up."

Harmer, aware now that if the constable would not take him into custody in the local jail, he would remain a prisoner of the settlers, shouted, "They got nuthin' on me, mister! Nuthin! You take care of me and git them outa here and back to their water-stealing settlement and I'll prove it to ya!"

A knot of curious people had begun to gather around as soon as they saw a prisoner lashed to a saddle. One of the men stepped forward and addressed Clayt.

"I'm Mike Whittaker, mister. I publish the local weekly. I know the constable. It's not the smartest thing I've ever done, but I got him appointed." He turned to the law officer.

"Boyd, this man is making a perfectly legal request of you. Now you help these folks out and witness the confession after it is signed." He paused. "Do it, Boyd!"

Clayt offered his hand. "I'm Clayton Adams." He indicated his companions. "This is Henry Deyer and his son, Oscar." Turning to the prisoner, he added, "And this man is Jake Harmer. He's foreman of the Gavilan spread downriver of us. He and two of his gunslingers murdered fourteen of our people and tried to blow up our Red Creek dam. There's more than enough water for all. The Gavilan's got new owners and it seems the new superintendent thinks he's going to need all of the water in the valley for his herds."

Sudden interest shone on Mike Whittaker's lean, aware face. "Well now, I don't exactly have to compete with the big city papers for stories around here, but every so often I file a telegraph cattle story for Horace Greeley in New York. Tell you what I'll do—I'll see that old Boyd here gets over his skittishness and witnesses the confession for you and I'll cosign it with him, just to make him comfortable." He raised a cautioning finger. "But there's a catch."

"What's that?" Clayt asked.

"That you give me the whole story, all the details—names, everything—and if it comes to a trial, which it probably should, I'll cover that, too, 'though I don't need any authority to do that. No matter which way it goes, I get all of the statements."

He paused and waited.

Clayt smiled. "Mr. Whittaker, if a handshake is a good enough contract, you've got it."

Obviously pleased, the newspaper publisher turned and said, "Alright, Mr. Constable, I'm going to invite all of us to my office. We'll look into a confession, see that it's all right and proper, then you and I are going to witness it, without prejudice, for these people."

* * *

A few doors north along the plaza, Clayt and Oss waited on their horses while Henry Deyer followed Mike Whittaker into the combination office and pressroom. The newsman cleared a table of a clutter of proofs. He pulled a compositor's stool close and indicated the lone chair. "Sit down and let me see the confession you set up."

Henry handed over the folded paper he had in his shirt pocket. The newsman studied it briefly and handed it back.

"It won't do the trick. You make it sound like that fellow out there acted entirely on his own. You mentioned new owners and a new superinteedant. Where are the owners from?"

"We understand one is from Chicago, a packer, and the other is an Englishman, Sir something-or-other."

Mike Whittaker's interest quickened.

"Well now," he said half to himself, "this could have the makings of a telegraph wire story." He looked across the table.

"Would you like me to see if I can come up with a confession that will cover the likelihoods?"

"Be much obliged," Henry replied.

Ten minutes passed while the newsman scribbled with a pen, crossed out, and rewrote. Finally, he handed the copy to Henry.

"See if this will cover it."

Henry read the clear sentences and handed the paper back with a wry smile. "There are a lot of things that I can do passing fair—cutting military orders and the like—but this kind of writing isn't one of them. You've got it all down and we thank you."

"Good! I'm going to make three copies and then let's get your man in here and see if he can be persuaded to sign them." He reached for some clean sheets and wiped the pen.

"Meantime, why don't you get him down. You've got him trussed up about as well as I've ever seen a hog tied."

By the time they finally got Harmer off the horse and hobbled, the newsman was just blotting the last of the copies. He looked up at Harmer whose bloodshot eyes were once again filled with savage defiance.

"I think these people are being more than fair with you, mister. If they are even telling half the truth, and I'd been the one to make the decision, I'd have had you swinging high weeks ago."

"Nobody's gonna stretch this neck! Least of any, these..."

Clayt drew his Smith and Wesson and prodded Harmer in the ribs. "I don't want to hear any more about stealing water or about the kind of people we are, Jake. And if you try one trick, we won't wait any longer for the marshall. We'll take you back and hang you like we should have done this morning."

"You'll never git me back there!" Harmer rasped. "You take me back to that stinkin' sweatbox, it'll be dead!"

"If that's how you want it, Jake, we'll be happy to accommodate you," Henry said with a dry smile.

"I won't sign no damned paper, I don't care what the writin' says. I didn't do nuthin' on my own. I had orders."

Mike Whittaker's eyebrows lifted in pleased surprise.

"Well now, that's a sort of confession in itself, Mr. Harmer. Would you care to elaborate—tell us who ordered you? Was it a man named T.K. Oakley, the name we have written down here?"

"He's the one!"

"Did he order you to kill these people and blow their dam?"

"He ordered me to do the job—fix it so they'd pull up stakes and git outa the territory."

"Did fixin' it include killing women and children?"

"I didn't kill no women and children! I never done such a terrible thing in my life!"

"You're a rotten-hearted liar!" Clayt snapped. "You and your hired gunslingers murdered my people in cold blood!"

"I didn't shoot 'em. Two hands I hired done it. I kilt them two myself, fur doin' it!"

Mike Whittaker picked up a copy of the confession. "This story's getting better by the minute. You're backing up everything these people have told me." He leaned forward, "In fact, Harmer, you are as good as dead right now, unless you can prove that this Oakley man ordered you to do everything that was done at Red Creek. If you can prove that, you may beat the gallows and spend the rest of your life in the territorial prison." He studied Harmer impersonally. "The choice is yours." He pushed the three copies across the table. "They'll untie your hand. Sign these and you live. Refuse and you'll surely be dead, and if I read these people rightly, you'll die in Red Creek."

Harmer stood breathing heavily. Pure rage burned in his eyes. Clayt watched him and waited for several minutes. When he saw signs of wavering, he started to rise.

"Alright, Jake, you've got one more minute." He glanced at the Seth Thomas clock. "When that hand comes up to the top, nothing's going to save your neck. You sign and pull Oakley into this with you, or you get your neck stretched all the way to hell and back. It's up to you. Personally, we all hope you swing."

Harmer's eyes darted from one to the other and back down to the papers. Breathing heavily, he let a few seconds pass. Finally, he blurted, "I'll sign 'em an' I'll see you all in hell!"

Jake Harmer scratched his labored signature on the copies and watched as they were witnessed.

"I'll keep one copy here in my safe," Whittaker said. "You'd better take the other two for your own safekeeping."

Clayt folded them and put them in his shirt pocket.

Harmer's free hand was bound again and he was returned to his horse. A crowd, much larger now, stood back asking each other half whispered questions that could not be answered.

Mike Whittaker waited until Clayt and the others were mounted. Then he sauntered over and rested a hand on Clayt's saddle skirt.

"A story without an end is not much of a story, Adams, so I'll help out a little. As soon as the marshall gets here, I'll tell him what happened—the confession and the rest. Then I'll send somebody down to tell you when it's time to bring this jasper in again. Just tell me how to get to your trail and I'll keep my word."

Well aware of the good it might do him as constable, Boyd Jones moved up beside him.

"I sure was glad to help, even it wasn't strictly in my line of duty," he said in a voice loud enough to be over-heard.

Before Clayt could reply, Mike Whittaker shot him an incredulous look and let out a derisive hoot.

"Good Gawd a'Mighty, Jones! I'll bet you a ten-cent cigar and throw in a bottle of Kentucky straight to boot that there's not another alleged lawman in the entire territory to match the likes of you!"

The constable grinned sheepishly and backed away as several bystanders guffawed.

When they passed the hotel on the way out of town, Buck Tanner hurried out to intercept them. He stabbed a finger at Harmer. "I see ya got ole Jake rigged out in some very becomin' ropes."

The foreman's mouth flew open.

"You was with 'em all the time, wasn't ya?" he blurted.

"I sure was," Buck agreed, "an' I'm mighty glad of it, too!"

Before Harmer could explode in a volcano of curses, Clayt drew his revolver and grasped it clublike by the barrel.

Dropping back from the lead he pushed in close to Harmer. "Keep your rotten mouth shut, Jake, or I'll bust your head wide open!" He raised the butt. "Shut up and stay shut up!" Harmer clamped his jaws and glowered in red-eyed hatred at both men.

Buck grinned and returned his attention to Clayt.

"I seen ya ridin' in but I was busy fixin' things up fur the new owners in the hotel. Garner and that Sir Charles fella come in on a special rig early this mornin'. Oakley's drivin' in with the surrey to pick 'em up. Should be along pretty quick now." He turned and glanced down the road. "We'll stop over t'night and ride back in the mornin'." A sudden thought amused him. "I reckon I'm ridin' shotgun in case there's a uprisin' of rattlesnakes or sumpthin.'

He stood with a hand raised as Clayt moved out with Oss behind him holding Harmer's halter lead. Henry Deyer, riding with his repeating rifle resting across the pommel, brought up the rear.

They had been on the road about a half hour when Clayt saw a dust cloud moving toward them. Slowing to a walk they rode on for another few minutes until they could make out a surrey drawn by two horses approaching at a good clip.

Clayt rode on ahead a bit and came back.

"It's Oakley alright. No use trying to avoid him. Let's meet him head on and settle it."

When Harmer recognized the ranch rig he was filled with grim elation. There was no question in his mind that when

Oakley saw him bound to the saddle there was sure to be a showdown. Depending on the first few minutes, if he figured out the right move, he could create a ruckus and cause Oakley to draw to defend him. In that case he could haze his horse and spoil Clayt's aim. It was three against one. The young guy was no gunslinger, and the old man would not be too fast with his rifle. T.K. would have a better-than-even chance to get all of them and he'd be free.

When his rig was close enough to identify the two men he thought were dead and buried, Oakley jerked the team to a stop and stood up.

"What in hell is going on here?" he shouted.

At the top of his lungs, Harmer screamed, "They trapped me, T.K.! Clay is one of 'em! They locked me up and then made me sign a paper that you and me is responsible for killin' them and blowin' their dam! I swear to God, T.K., they made me sign the papers!"

"Are you telling me they made you sign a confession?" Oakley asked as, very subtly, he eased the flap of his long black dress coat open and urged the team closer.

"As God is my witness, T.K.—in front of the constable and a guy who prints newspapers in Vegas!"

Oakley's eyes swept across the men from Red Creek.

"Where's the paper? Let's see what you signed."

"He's got it!" Harmer cried, twisting in the saddle to nod at Clayt.

Oakley shook his head. "I don't believe you're that stupid, Jake."

"If you want some proof," Clayt said, reaching into his pocket for one of the folded confessions, "here it is." He held it out. Oakley hesitated for a moment, fearing a trap, then reached for it warily with his left hand.

He read it several times, then wagged his head in disbelief and smiled. Very slowly, he reached into the top pocket of his brocade vest and removed a match. Leaning forward, with the confession in his left hand, he scratched the match on the dashboard and set fire to a corner. When it caught, he angled the paper until it was fully aflame then dropped it into the dust alongside the surrey.

"Well," he said with a satisfied smile, "I guess that settles this nonsense, doesn't it?"

"He's got more of 'em!" Harmer yelled in a hoarse voice, "He's got two more!"

Alarmed now, Oakley glanced at Clayt.

"He's right, T.K.—two more of them, all signed and witnessed, and stored in a safe in town." Oakley tensed and his eyes, calculating now, darted from one to the other. Suddenly the skirt of his long black coat flew aside.

"Don't do it!" Clayt shouted, but too late. Oakley's ivory-handled six-gun appeared from nowhere and swung point-blank at Harmer. Before he could pull the trigger, Clayt drew and shot the gun from his hand. In the next instant, Harmer kicked his heels into his mount. The startled animal bolted to the left, pulling the halter lead from Oss's grip. Henry shouted a warning as Oakley drew a second revolver from his belt. The first shot missed Harmer and struck the wildly dodging horse in the right rump as it raced across the mesa. The animal stumbled as Harmer, helpless to guide it, kept kicking it savagely. Oakley's second shot went wild when Clayt spurred his animal broadside into the team, jerking the rig. A third shot from Oakley's numbed hand seemed to have hit Harmer in the lower back. His scream could be heard across the mesa as he continued to punish the animal.

Without warning, Oakley swung toward Clayt. Before he could pull the trigger, a forty-four caliber slug from Henry Deyer's repeating rifle exploded through Oakley's chest. For an instant he remained upright, then slowly his legs buckled and his long body collapsed and sagged over the seat back.

Stunned for a moment, Clayt recovered, shouted to Oss to follow, and raced off across the mesa in pursuit. They could see Harmer, still bound securely to the saddle, trying to stay upright as the animal dodged through the thick scrub growth of oak, piñon, and sage.

Urging their own mounts to the utmost, Clayt and Oss managed to gain a little ground by riding as straight as possible. They could see Harmer clearly now. His lower back was bleeding.

"He's been hit pretty bad," Clayt called across to Oss. "There's no way he can control that animal. If we don't catch him he can die on us before we get him to the law."

"At least Oakley's out of the way now," Oss shouted.

"He is, but we still don't know anything about the new owners. If Oakley took his orders from them, there's still a mess of trouble. We need Jake alive. If he talks he can stop them."

They were still gaining a little when suddenly they saw Harmer's horse slide to a brace-legged stop and wheel left.

"It's got to be a deep barranca," Clayt called. "Let's angle north a little!"

They'd gone only a few yards when Oss shouted. "Look at that! Harmer's horse! No saddle!"

Both men pulled up to a rearing stop and stared after the animal that had now doubled back toward the road.

"That saddle didn't just fall off!" Clayt said. "It had a double cinch! Come on. Let's see what happened."

They had moved only a few yards when Oss pointed off to his left. "Good God, Clayt! Look!"

Clayt pulled up short and followed his arm. For an instant he did not believe his eyes. Only partially visible through the dense stand of piñon, they saw Harmer apparently suspended in midair, still lashed to the saddle.

Dismounting, both men ran into the thicket, let out shocked cries, and stopped, staring in mute horror as Harmer's thick body jerked in spasmodic death throes. Protruding from his back was the sharp, jagged, spearlike point of an old, sun-hardened piñon limb that had impaled him. Glistening in the sun were elastic strands of gut that had been forced out with the point.

Oss turned away, on the verge of nausea. "Great God," he gasped, "what a horrible way for anything to die!"

Clayt moved up close and forced himself to look. As he watched, Harmer's head lolled onto his shoulder and blood began spilling down his cheek. Clayt spat and his hand moved to the butt of the Smith and Wesson. For a moment he considered doing what he would do for any mortally wounded animal but the need ended when Harmer's body gave one last violent shudder and he was gone.

He turned away and walked back to Oss.

"Mount up and see if you can catch his horse. If you can't we'll double up on mine and take him back on yours."

When Oss hesitated, Clayt insisted. "Go on now! I'll get him down and cut him loose. When you get back we'll put him across his saddle—or yours. Go on now, Oss. Please."

Oss hesitated for a moment, then turned, glad to leave. When he was out of sight Clayt remounted. Riding close, he looped one end of his seldom used rawhide lariat over the base of the limb and secured it. Then, taking a turn around his saddle horn, he urged his horse to pull until the brittle old limb snapped and fell to the ground with its gruesome burden.

Closing his eyes as he grasped the deadly piece, he pulled

it free of Harmer's body, walked off a few yards, and threw it as far as he could. Grimacing at the thought, he visualized the animals that would sniff it out and fight over it in the night.

Chapter Sixteen

It was well past noon when Henry, driving the rig with its macabre cargo lashed on the back seat, rolled into the plaza with Clayt and Oss riding alongside. The old fellow who guarded the express office saw them first. Uttering a wheezing, "Whoo—ee!" he scooted into two adjoining doorways to pass the news. By the time the rig pulled to a stop in front of the newspaper office, customers, store keepers, women, and children were converging on the plaza.

Clayt quieted them down a little with raised hands. When the clamor of questions subsided enough to be heard he said, "The dirty business that brought us to town a couple of hours ago just got settled back there." He indicated the road with a nod. "The man who murdered our people and the man who set him to it, are both here...." He pointed to the bodies covered by Oakley's long coat. "The one who did the killing killed himself by accident. The other one got killed trying to shut him up." His eyes moved across the faces and came to rest on the bartender whose information had set them on the right track. Pointing, he said, "Sorry I don't know this man's name, but we can thank him for helping us find the mad coyotes."

As he hoped it would, the attention was diverted to the

bartender who by now was wearing his importance on his sleeve.

Wiping ink from his hands, Mike Whittaker pushed through the crowd. He regarded the tacit answers to his question that were loaded in the surrey, then looked up at Clayt.

"We'll put them in the town morgue, but you-all had better come inside first."

Henry Deyer shook his head. "I'll wait here. Oss will go look for the constable." A voice on the edge of the crowd called, "He's comin' now."

The newspaper man craned his neck and pushed out to meet him.

"What's goin' on?" Boyd Jones asked.

"What's going on," Mike Whittaker replied, "is some business for your town morgue."

The constable thrust out his cushioned chin. "Now you lookee here, Mike, I already done more'n I should of. I ain't gonna store no stiffs in my shed. Who are they and who's gonna put 'em down?"

"They're better stiffs than you usually stash there, Jones, and you're going to keep them there until some proper disposition can be made."

When the constable started to protest again, the newspaper publisher reached out and tapped the badge. "You're going to do that, Boyd Jones, if I have to swear that the killing took place right here in town. That'll make it your business." He gave the badge another poke. "You stay here and come on inside while we figure out what to do!"

They had been in the cluttered little office for only a minute or two when Buck Tanner came running up from the hotel. He pushed his way close enough to the surrey to see what had happened then looked anxiously up at Henry, still on the seat. "Are you folks alright?" he asked.

"None of ours got hurt, Buck."

154

"Thank God fur that! Where are they?"

"Inside."

Without waiting, he pushed his way through to the door and entered. Mike Whittaker looked at him and frowned.

"Who are you?"

Before Buck could answer, Clayt broke in. "He's a friend, Mr. Whittaker. A good friend. He's the trail boss at the Gavilan. Buck Tanner."

The publisher's eyebrows lifted. "Well now, seems I have got a big city story!" Turning to Buck, he said, "How do you figure in this? Those two out there were your bosses. Right?"

"Yes sir. That's right—only now you might say they *was* my bosses. I've got new ones now—down at the hotel." Without waiting for another question, Buck turned to Clayt. "I think mebbe ya oughta talk to 'em, Clay. They don't know none of this yet."

"I want to talk to them," Clayt replied, "just as soon as we're through here." He reached over and gave Buck's shoulder a friendly squeeze. "Do something for me. Go back to the hotel and tell them I need to see them. Don't tell them what's happened yet. I want to ask them some questions. I need to know if they had any hand in this."

Buck's sun-squinted eyes reflected real concern. He ducked his head uncertainly.

"My guess is they's not the kind, Clay. Leastwise, that's how I figger 'em right now."

"Go on anyway, Buck. Set it up. I'll tell you what happened before I talk to them. I'll be there in a little bit."

Buck left immediately. When the door closed behind him Mike Whittaker turned to Clayt and to Oss who had come in with the constable.

"I take it the 'they' you're talking about are the new owners, the Chicago packer and the titled Englishman?"

"That's right."

"Do you know their names?" A pen was poised as he asked.

"Garner and a Sir Charles—I didn't get the last name. You can get them for yourself and ask some other questions if you want. I'd like you there." He nodded toward the rig. "Let's get them under cover first."

Mike Whittaker shook his head. "They'll keep for a few minutes more. First give me a rundown on what happened."

While the publisher took notes, Clayt described the events of the past hour. When he finished, Mike Whittaker relaxed and rubbed his cramped fingers. Blotting the scrawled notes, he said, "All of a sudden I believe in divine retribution!"

The publisher questioned Clayt and Oss for another ten minutes, while the constable grunted and fidgeted, then he put aside his notes.

"That'll do it for now. I can get the rest of the story—if there is any—from the new owners."

Outside, Mike Whittaker took Boyd Jones by the arm.

"Mr. Constable," he said loud enough for the crowd of curious citizens to hear, "Mr. Constable, why don't you climb up in the rig and ride the gentlemen over to your morgue shed?"

The local lawman pulled free. "I ain't ridin' with no corpses! That there's 'Digger's' job. I'm walkin' and they can folla!"

Mike Whittaker turned to Clayt. "'Digger,' is Billy Donahoo. He runs the feed store, but lately he's been doing better as the undertaker. Five dollars a corpse, including the digging, but no marker. The concerned can put up their own."

Henry glanced back at his unwelcome passengers and cursed under his breath. "Let's get on with it. They're beginning to stiffen up. I'll put out the ten dollars but I want them down tonight, or in the cool of the morning."

The constable, already a few steps away, stopped. "They'll

be down t'night. In this weather I'd a lot rather have 'em low than high!''

Clayt turned to Oss. "Ride with your father and give him a hand. I'll be back here in a half hour and tell you what happened. I want to ride back this afternoon.''

Unhappy, Oss climbed into the rig. Clayt and Mike Whittaker watched as the crowd gave way to let the surrey pass. A few bystanders followed behind to get a look at the corpses.

"They've seen enough of them around here this past year or so," the publisher observed, "but I'll never understand why they want a close look.''

"Where Harmer's concerned," Clayt said, "they'd better have strong stomachs!''

Buck Tanner was waiting for them in front of the hotel.

"They're in the bar," he said. "I didn't tell 'em they're fresh out of a superintendent an' a foreman.''

"Do they know what you do?" Clayt asked.

"I told 'em I was the oldest hand on the spread, trail boss. They remembered 'cause I drove 'em when they first come here.''

"Have they asked where Oakley is...or when he's coming in?''

Buck Tanner shook his head. "Nope. But I was ready fur 'em...in case. I figgered to not say anythin' 'cept that Oakley was some delayed.''

Mike Whittaker managed a dry smile. "In a land of understatement, Mr. Tanner, you've just won a prize.''

The old trail boss frowned and cocked his head, then shrugged. "I do thank ya," he said somewhat uncertainly.

Clayt put a hand on Buck's shoulder and urged him to the bar.

They found the new owners seated at a table for four toward the back. Clayt remembered the table. The bartender who had been at the newspaper office was not there. An older man with rheumy eyes and a bulbous nose spiderwebbed with tiny varicose veins, presided.

When the new owners saw Buck enter, they rose smiling. The shorter of the two men reached for a fifth chair and pulled it close. Signaling, he called, "Come have a seat."

Buck's introductions were straight to the point.

"Folks," he said, "shake hands with Clay Adams. He wants t'talk to ya." Turning to Mike Whittaker, he was equally to the point. "I only jes met this gentleman. He prints the newspaper but you kin shake with him too. He's a friend."

Clayt saw a flicker of concern in both men's eyes. The new owner from Chicago extended a hand. "I'm Tom Garner and this is my partner, Sir Charles Freebairn." The Englishman's smile was open and very friendly. Indicating the chairs, he said, "Please be seated, gentlemen. We're very happy to have an opportunity to talk with you." He motioned to the bartender. "My good man," he called in a pleasantly deep, well-modulated voice, "will you see what our friends will have to drink?"

Clayt and Mike Whittaker both ordered beers. When Buck glanced at Clayt uncomfortably, Sir Charles laughed softly.

"Perhaps our Mister Tanner would prefer something with...uh...a bit more authority?"

Relieved to be included, Buck held up a staying hand.

"Thankee, sir. I'll jes' wet my whistle with a little beer. I save whiskey fur snake bites and weddin's—which I've neither had any truck with so fur."

Tom Garner smiled across the table. "Well, Buck, you're off to a good start with us, at least. When do you expect T.K. Oakley?"

Buck Tanner swallowed hard and looked uncomfortable.

"Mr. Tanner," Clayt began, "You and..." When he

hesitated and glanced at the other owner, the Englishman's smile broadened.

"Sir Charles will do, Mr. Adams."

"You and Sir Charles," Clayt continued, "are not going to be happy with the news today. That is why I asked Mike Whittaker to join us. He can confirm some of the details."

Tom Garner and Sir Charles exchanged fleeting glances. Turning back to Clayt, Garner said, "Well, life in our business is not without surprises. What's happened?"

Clayt laid it on the table without apparent emotion.

"Your man Oakley and his foreman, Jake Harmer, are dead." Both Clayt and Whittaker expected a shocked reaction. Instead, the new owners showed not the least surprise. Tom Garner, a strongly built, smooth-shaven man in his middle years, brushed a lock of black wavy hair from his forehead and nodded. The Englishman's eyebrows lifted slightly but nothing else could be read on his clean-lined, aristocratic face.

Finally, after a long pause, he leaned forward.

"Do I understand, Mr. Adams, that their demise was rather recent—and unexpected?"

Clayt's eyes moved from one to the other and he settled himself in the chair.

"You will understand very clearly, gentlemen, when you hear why and when all of this happened. And if you have any doubts about the 'why' part of it"—he reached into his pocket and pulled out the remaining confession—"I think this paper will clear it up."

Garner, concerned now, reached for the paper.

"Let me see it, Adams."

Clayt continued to hold it for a moment. "The paper's a confession, signed by your recent foreman, and what he confessed to will also clear up Oakley's part in the matter."

Garner read the confession through twice and handed it to Sir Charles. The Englishman's expression underwent a slow change to near disbelief. He took his time handing it back to Clayt.

"I think you should have your say, Mr. Adams, and I assure you, you'll have an attentive audience. Go on, please."

The drinks sat untouched as Clayt began at the beginning. He described the trip up from Texas after the war, the establishing of the colony and its purpose, the peaceful life that his father and Henry Deyer had dedicated them all to live, the building of the dam, just large enough to meet their own simple irrigation requirements, and the feeling of accomplishment that came with the passing years.

The men listened, engrossed. Not wishing to distract by taking notes, Mike Whittaker made careful mental notes that he meant to confirm later.

During Clayt's simple description of the horror of the night attack and the wanton slaughter of men, women, and children, Sir Charles could not conceal his shock. "Horrible!" he whispered. "Unbelievable!" Several times he asked, "In the name of God, why?" Tom Garner, head lowered and eyes closed, sat lost in thought.

When Clayt recited the events that led to his decision to hire on to confirm Harmer's guilt, Buck Tanner's head nodded in agreement. Clayt made it clear to the new owners that his only purpose was to satisfy his people of Harmer's guilt, to fix the responsibility of anyone else involved, and to see that they were properly prosecuted under the law.

"In the end," he said, "we did not take the law into our hands. We kept our pledge to my father. We proved Harmer's guilt, and Oakley's. Oakley tried to kill Harmer to keep him from talking. When Harmer seemed to be getting away, he turned his gun on me and Henry Deyer was forced to kill him. We would have much preferred the law did that for us. We want an end to violence." He made a fist and struck it sharply on the table. "We mean to have it!"

He had been talking for nearly a half hour and his throat

was parched. Some of the old outrage had come back with the retelling. When he reached for the warm beer, the others eased back, sat for a moment without words, then reached for their own drinks.

The silence was broken by Sir Charles. He set his stein on the table and pushed it away. After a long moment of introspection he glanced at Tom Garner then back to Clayt.

"Mr. Adams," he began in a tone that Clayt felt could not be other than sincere, "Tom and I see eye to eye on most things and I can assure you, that we'll see as one on this matter."

He paused to gather his words. "First of all, let me say, there can be no thought that a price in gold can ever be put on a human life by honorable people. Tom and I are honorable people, honorable in business and in our personal dealings. That can be easily confirmed. That is why I say that we will insist on doing all possible to reimburse you and your people for the physical damage Oakley and Harmer inflicted on you. But do understand that in doing so, we are in no way attempting to assuage your grief or make reparations for the loss of your loved ones. We knew nothing of Harmer. We knew Oakley for the expert cattleman he apparently was. Beyond that, we knew nothing of his personal life. Harmer was his choice. We wanted him to be easy with the men he would have to rely on. That is just good business practice. Apparently, on that count, we have made a ghastly mistake. There are no words to express our shock and our sorrow." He paused and looked deeply into Clayt's eyes, cold and still reflecting remembered pain and anger. "I beg you, Mr. Adams, to believe that as the truth before God."

The meeting ended in silence. Another round of beer was brought to the table but each man drank slowly, without relish. There were no easy words.

Clayt felt that he had made it plain that if the new owners had been in any way responsible for Oakley's decision, they would have to answer, too. The confession was all that would be required to bring them to court. Under oath they would either clear themselves or suffer the consequences. But even as he considered that possibility, he could not bring himself to believe that either Garner or the Englishman would resort to what amounted to insane violence to get their way.

Clayt glanced outside and saw Henry and Oss driving up in the ranch rig. It was midafternoon, later than he wanted to start back, but he was anxious to get home. He turned to Buck.

"Henry will turn the team over to you now. We're going to ride back to Red Creek. We'll return the Gavilan horses tomorrow or the next day."

Before Buck could reply, Tom Garner spoke up. "You keep those animals, Clayton. They're yours now."

"We insist," Sir Charles broke in. "If they're good mounts, you keep them."

"You heard the gentlemen, Clay," Buck said. "You keep that little buckskin that the girl rode off, too. We got a good *caballada.* Enough fur now."

"I trust Tanner's judgment," Garner added. "You keep any ranch stock you've been riding. Don't bring it around."

Buck turned to him. "I do thank ya, Mr. Garner." He cocked his head and squinted at Clayt. "Only one thing—I know you like t'be called 'Clayt—with a 't' on the end—and I hope you'll be easy until I git used to puttin' it there."

Clayt pushed back his chair. "With or without the 't' Buck, you're one of the best men I know. You remember what I said to you. You will always be welcomed at Red Creek— for as long as you want to stay."

Sir Charles rose, smiling. "I don't want to impose my will on Buck," he said, "but I'm sure he's going to be needed and equally welcome at the Gavilan—just as you will be, Clayt with a 't.'"

The small joke eased the air. Tom Garner came around

the table and offered his hand. "Unless Buck has other plans, he's going to have important work at the Gavilan. Very important," he said, "and that goes for you too, Clayt. We hope to have reason to see you soon." He turned to Mike Whittaker. "I'm very glad that you could be with us, Mike. We'll answer your questions about our plans—and none of them have anything to do with disturbing the peace here or anywhere else. We hope you'll come to believe that."

The publisher nodded and smiled. "I find I sort of tend to."

Chapter Seventeen

They had pushed their animals on the return trip. It was well after sundown when they stopped at the top of the trail and "hallooed." Immediately settlers began emerging from their homes carrying lanterns. By the time the three riders reached the bottom of the trail and crossed the dam, the last of the settlers had entered the big meeting house.

Mary was waiting for them with Nelda and Kate. When she saw Oss leading Harmer's horse with its empty saddle, she breathed a great sigh of relief.

"Oh, Clayt! Thank God you turned that filthy beast over to the law!" Nodding toward the meeting house, she added, "They're all there, full of fidgets and waiting to hear what happened. But I've kept your suppers warm. I want you to wash up and eat first."

Clayt turned questioning eyes to Henry and Oss.

"We'll eat some later," he replied, "after we've talked. We'd rather get the telling done first."

Henry nodded. "Oss and I will put up the horses and wash. We'll meet you over there." Clayt eased out of the saddle and handed the reins to him. Disappointed, Mary nodded to the girls. "Things will keep for an hour or so." Turning to Nelda, she said, "Why don't you get some towels for your brother?"

Clayt stripped off his shirt and shook a small cloud of dust from it. While he was plunging his face and most of his head in the small wash trough, Mary brushed it and shook it some more. When he half submerged his upper body one last time and came up blowing, both girls laughed.

Nelda forced a towel into his groping hands and put a second one over his dripping shoulders.

"You sound like an old bull in a buff wallow," she said. Clayt's response was muffled in the towel.

Refreshed, he gave his shirt one last shake and pulled it on. A few minutes later, followed by his mother and the girls, he entered the meeting house. Somehow, the lanterns hanging from their pegs around the walls, seemed brighter than usual.

Oss had been holding places on the front bench for them. Henry was waiting at the lectern. When they were seated, he looked over the assembled settlers. Finally he spoke in a voice rough with fatigue. "I'm suffering some from a troubled conscience. This afternoon, I had to break our pledge to Asa." He paused and let his eyes wander over the up-turned faces. "I'm not going to apologize."

"If you killed Harmer you don't have to!" a voice shouted. Ignoring the man, Henry continued, "A lot of things could have changed today. We're not sure yet. But that's for Clayt to tell you"—he paused again and began to move from the platform—"which he is going to do now."

Moving slowly, Clayt stepped up on the platform and took his place behind the lectern. Since his father's death it had been Henry Deyer's territory. Now some, including Henry himself, were saying that it was his place. It was not a place that he would ever aspire to occupy.

Clutching the edge of the lectern, he looked down at his mother and sister and at Oss and Kate. When Henry took a place beside them, he deliberately studied the anxious faces. For the first time since the tragedy wreaked on them by

Harmer, he saw a glimmer of hope in eyes dulled by fear, anger, and sorrow without end.

Speaking matter-of-factly, he recited the events just as they had happened from the time they had ridden into Las Vegas in search of the marshall. As their frustration had mounted with each new obstacle, those who could not yet know the result of the trip murmured in sympathy and shared frustration.

Though he made no attempt to dramatize the climax of the trip, anticipation mixed with rising anxiety brought the settlers to the edge of their benches. In spite of himself, Clayt's voice tightened as he told of the encounter with Oakley, the burning of the confession, the superintendent's attempt to kill Harmer to keep from being incriminated, and his final end as Henry's rifle slug saved their lives.

Fervent "Thank Gods" mingled with anxious questions as men called, "What happened to Harmer? Did you kill him, too?"

Clayt held up a hand for quiet.

"No, we didn't kill him. We didn't have to. The Good Lord took a hand in that."

Pressed for details, Clayt decided to spare them nothing. When he finished, the room was dead silent as each one who had suffered at Jake Harmer's hands, or who had comforted others who had, said their own private prayers of gratitude.

Clayt straightened on the lectern and seemed about to leave when Jakob Gruen stood up.

"Henry said a lot of things could have changed today but you're not sure yet? Do you mean you don't know about the new owners and whether or not they had a hand in it?"

Clayt turned to Henry. "Am I right when I say that they seemed very upset when they heard what happened?"

"I judged them to be," he replied. "Also, Buck Tanner's known them since they bought up the place. He figures them for decent people."

Clayt nodded. "And so does Mike Whittaker apparently."

"What about you, Clayt?" his mother asked.

Clayt took his own time answering. "I'd like to believe that. It would mean an end to our trouble, but I want to do a little more nosing around."

Mary's expression changed from hope to grave concern. "Don't tell me you're going to go riding down there again!"

"I am," Clayt replied. "They said we could keep their horses. They also said they would pay us for the damage to the dam. I want to listen to them talk some more before I fix them in my mind."

Thad Jones, whose shoulder had been shattered by a rifle slug, jumped up.

"Don't you be a damned fool, Clayton Adams! Money don't mean a thing to the likes of them. Neither does talk. They hired Oakley to run their spread. They sure knew what kind of a snake he was!"

A scattering of voices called, "Hear! Hear!"

Clayt could have told them what he had been told by both Garner and Sir Charles, that beyond the fact that T.K. Oakley was known as a top cattle man, they knew nothing of him. He did not want to sound as though he was defending them when, in fact, he was unsettled in his own mind.

"I'll take the horses back and listen to them talk some more. That's all I've got to say tonight."

Ignoring other persistent questions, he joined his mother and the others and left the meeting house.

Henry and Oss thanked Mary for keeping their supper. When they rose to leave, Mary stopped them.

"Henry, I listened to the talk. Nobody blamed you for breaking your pledge to Asa. You didn't take the law into your hands. You killed a killer to save your own life and your son's and mine." She took both of his hands in hers.

"You are being blessed, Henry, by me, by all of us—and by my Asa, too. Believe that."

While the women were straightening up the kitchen, Clayt wandered outside. Needing some time alone, he picked his way through the darkness along the familiar trail to the corral. He would take the horses back but he would offer to buy his own chestnut and the little buckskin that Kate loved. He knew that if Garner and his wealthy English backer had been lying there was little or no chance that he would be able to mark the truth. Probably the best he could do would be to let them understand that the secure confession signed by Harmer, implicating Oakley could, by inference, implicate them, too. With thousands of dollars at stake in the Gavilan, it seemed reasonable to assume that they would chose to become good neighbors. In any case he found some comfort in old Buck's assessment of them.

At the corral Clayt climbed up and perched on the top rail. He had been there only scant minutes when he heard a soft whinny and footsteps behind him. He turned just as the little buckskin mare came up to nuzzle his shoulder.

He ran his hand over its velvety nose. "You did a good job, girl," he said half aloud. As he continued to caress her his mind ran back to that earlier night at the Gavilan corral and to the surprising and dangerous situation that developed when, on impulse, he decided to save an unknown girl from Oakley's abuse. Beyond seeing her at a distance hanging out the wash, and closer up when she served him coffee during his talk with the superintendent, he knew nothing of her. She was young and she had been badly used before she came to the Gavilan, but she had felt like a woman in his arms when he carried her to the barn. His mother and sister had worked wonders with her. Loving care had brought with it a near miraculous change. Now she was every bit as pretty as Nelda, and getting prettier.

"Kate comes from strong stock," his mother had said.

"She had to, to come through what she's suffered." Clayt thought the same could be said of them all. Only the strong survived in the territory. His thoughts turned to Hazel. She had been pretty, too. Beautiful was a better word, but too finely wrought, too fragile. When he had proposed and held her to kiss her, he had been forced to restrain himself lest she shatter in his arms like fine porcelain.

In the house Mary watched Nelda and Kate finishing the dishes as she folded flat-dried linen. What a blessed addition to the family Kate was, she thought. No one could ever take the place of Fern, whose death had been merciful only in its suddenness. The thought brought the threat of tears, and a second thought sent them brimming. Mary felt again Kate's poor little body cradled in her arms with her head against her own motherly bosom as she had listened to the girl's description of her father's death at the hands of the renegade Indian raiders and her treatment as their human chattel until she was traded to the comancheros and then sold to Oakley. The recollection brought an inward shudder and a wordless prayer of thanks that now, perhaps, there would be an end to fear, a chance to go on, a chance for time to dull the pain and do its healing.

With Clayt as his father's successor, and with Henry as the wise elder, life could be good again—almost as good as Asa and Henry dreamed it would be—because their son would bring the community his father's strength and leadership. Clayt could hold them together. She had seen that confirmed again tonight.

When the kitchen work was finished, Kate stood in the doorway for a few minutes enjoying the cool breeze coming down the canyon, cooler still for having ruffled the surface of the refilled pond. She loved the night sounds. The canyon was filled with them: melodic calls of night birds, the soft rush of the water through the new spillway, the musical babbling as it was freed to run again over the smoothed boulders, the hollow croaking of the bullfrogs in the reeds along the pond, the rhythmic rasping of the courting cicadas, and the hollow, metallic clanking of cowbells in the long, narrow pastures on either side of the creek.

Clayt would be out there in the night, alone with his thoughts, unwinding after a day that must have spelled the future of the entire Red Creek settlement.

Just beyond the lamp glow from the open door a large chopping block offered a seat. She rested on it briefly, enjoying the vagrant fingers of breeze that teased the hair against her cheek. Then, unaccountably, she felt the need to pet the little buckskin mare. She moved across the yard's hard-packed earth and picked her way through the darkness down the trail to the corral and barns. Above her the black rim of the canyon sliced across the luminous, starlit sky.

When she was within a few yards of the corral the mare heard her coming and whinnyed softly. Clayt scratched its ear. "Sounds like company's coming," he said.

Kate let out a startled little cry and moved several steps closer until she could make out the tall figure perched above her.

"Oh, Clayt," she said. "I'm sorry. I didn't know you were here." When she turned to leave Clayt stopped her.

"Seems corrals are where you and I are supposed to meet. Climb up here and scratch your friend's ear."

Kate climbed up high enough to brace her arms on the top rail. In her eagerness for attention, the mare nudged her and nearly upset her. Recovering, she put an arm around the animal's neck and rested her cheek against it.

"I have a lot to thank you for, little lady," she said in a soft voice. "More than I can ever say." Without looking at him she added, "And more to thank you for, Clayt, and your people."

"It's ours to thank you, too, Kate," Clayt replied, trying without much success to conceal a recurring emotion that he had been trying to deny ever since he had found himself caring about what happened to the girl. Its persistence annoyed him: Part of it was a sense of guilt. The emotion was so like that he had felt for Hazel from the first, a feeling that had turned to bitterness and pain with her passing. He was through with such feelings, he told himself. Trouble! Never again!

An awkward silence had ensued before Kate climbed down to give the mare a goodbye petting. Clayt eased off the rail and dropped down beside her.

"We hope you'll stay with us, Kate. It means so much to us...to Mom and Nelda...." He cussed himself inwardly for fumbling around with the words. He could not see Kate's wry smile.

"I know," she replied, "I'm very lucky—I mean, we all are—you being here safe now, means so much to everybody." Recalling what he had said to her earlier, "I guess Red Creek is getting a little tight around the shoulders for me lately. Maybe it's time I got out and looked around a little," she forced out self-serving words that she was unable to contain.

"Everybody is praying that you'll take your father's place now. They need somebody to look up to—to make them feel safe. You do that—for everybody."

She thought his silence meant that he was annoyed but when she started to move away he caught her arm and linked it through his. She hesitated, then removed it gently. He pretended not to notice. Instead, he placed a hand in the middle of her back. "Come on," he said, "I'll walk you. I'm going to fill the woodbox and turn in. This has been more day than I need."

At the house, Kate found Mary and Nelda seated at the table having a goodnight cup of Mormon Tea, made from the mesa plant's leafless stems. Refusing a cup for herself, she sat across the table from them but something in her manner discouraged much talk. Clayt had left her at the door and disappeared in the direction of the community woodpile. Ten minutes later when he returned to drop the load in the box, he too, seemed strangely removed. He stood for a moment, then gave them a cursory nod. "I've used up this day," he said. "I'll see you in the morning."

Chapter Eighteen

Three days after Jake Harmer and T.K. Oakley had been buried in rough pine coffins in the unclaimed deceased section of the Las Vegas cemetery, Mike Whittaker ran a front-page story describing in detail the events that had terminated in the deaths of the Gavilan superintendent and his foreman. In a box he reproduced Harmer's confession. He ended the story by reporting that the Gavilan's new owners, Tom Garner of Chicago, Illinois, and Sir Charles Freebairn of London, England, had offered to pay reparations to the Red Creek settlers and, as a gesture of "Christian concern," had ordered two wooden crosses bearing the names of the pair and date of death erected at the grave sites. Sir Charles was quoted as saying, "We feel it is only common decency that the resting places of these two men be properly marked in the event relatives wish to locate them and take their remains to a final resting place. We regret deeply the actions that have tarnished the Gavilan name and wish to reassure everyone in the territory that under our new owner- ship, violence will never play a part in the operation of the ranch."

On the fifth day Buck Tanner paid a surprise visit to the

settlement. He had started before sunrise and he seemed excited.

"I ain't stayin'," he told Clayt, as Henry and Oss and several of the others gathered around. "I'm ridin' back just as soon's I water my horse. Tom Garner and Sir Charles is hopin' that you'll come ridin' back with me. They sent me to tell ya they want mightily to talk to ya."

"About what?" Clayt asked.

The old trail boss shrugged. "Durned if I know. They took a lot of time askin' me questions about ya, but they sure didn't tell me what fur. They's friendly enough," he added, "but they sure play close to the vest."

Clayt studied Buck Tanner long enough to make the old man uncomfortable.

"I truly don't know what's on their mind, Clayt," he added defensively, "But I figgered it might have sumpthin' to do with makin' things right with you and your people here."

"They offered and I turned them down," Clayt replied.

Tanner nodded. "I know. But I do know they want you to keep the horses."

"I'll buy the buckskin and the chestnut," Clayt said, "but I don't want Harmer's piebald. You can take it back with you."

Buck Tanner ducked his head in resigned agreement. "If that's how you want it, but I sure wish you'd ride back with me. You'd only have to stay long 'nuf to do some talkin'. Like I said, Clayt, they sure don't ask me to set in on their powwows, but I'll stake my life on one thing, 'less I've plumb forgot how to size up a man, it's nuthin' bad!"

Clayt pondered for a moment, then excused himself and went into the house.

"Mom, will you and the girls set out some coffee and biscuits for Buck Tanner? I want to talk privately with Henry and Oss for a few minutes. I'll come in and have a cup with him in a bit."

In the yard again, Clayt took Buck's reins and tied them to a ring post. The old trail boss cocked an eyebrow.

"You gonna git ready to ride?"

"I don't know yet, Buck. You go inside. Mom and the girls have some coffee and biscuits for you. I'll be there in a minute."

Still a bit puzzled, Buck stomped his boots and undid his chaps.

"Hang them on that peg by the door," Clayt said as he turned toward the others who were waiting a few yards away.

"You heard him. What do you make of it?" he asked as he approached them.

Henry fingered the short stubble of beard. Finally he looked up. "'Better safe than sorry' keeps running through my mind."

"I know," Clayt said, "but I don't see any danger down there now. I trust Buck and I need to know more about those new owners."

Jakob Gruen, who had walked over still carrying a silversmith's hammer, wagged it for emphasis.

"Say what you want, Clayt, but you can't always tell about a man from his looks or his words. I'm an expert! My darling little wife and I got taken in by such a man—John Henry Noyes. He started Oneida Colony. He had the notion that men with pretty wives should make them mate with the strongest men in the community in order to produce a super-race of people. He looked like the finest gentleman you could ever meet, but he was for breaking nine of the Ten Commandments as our sacred duty!" He wagged his head. "You can't tell!"

Clayt tried hard to keep from smiling. Noyes was the reason Jakob and Hilde had deserted and come west.

"I think they're only interested in breeding cattle at the Gavilan," he said, "and making money. What I want to do is find out just how far they are likely to go to do that."

"How long will you be gone?" Oss asked.

"If I ride now I should be back tomorrow around sundown."

Henry nodded. "I know you're set to ride, Clayt, so why don't we say that if you're not back by then, one of us will be looking to see why?"

John Bates, who had been standing quietly, listening, stepped closer. "I'll make a guess. Those men won't try to get what they want with bullets. They'll try with dollars. I'll bet they're going to make a proposition to buy us out, take over everything—the houses, the barns, the water—everything. If they're thinking of thousand-head herds, they'll need out-camps. They can put gathering pens up on top and feed the range stock around here into the main drive."

"If that's what they have in mind," Jakob asked, "what would you say, Clayt?"

"It's not my say." He turned to Henry. "You'd call a meeting and put it to a vote I expect?"

"I would," he agreed.

"I'm not 'specially speaking for me," Jakob put in, "but there are some who would still take off for a share of the money—even with Harmer and Oakley dead and gone."

"They could do that," Clayt agreed, "if there was enough money to make it worthwhile—and if the decision was to sell out."

Henry was growing impatient. He waved a hand. "Let's quit this palaver! Clayt knew he was going before he asked us. The sooner he goes, the sooner we know."

Henry and Oss followed Clayt inside.

Addressing the women, he said, "I don't want to hear any hemming and hawing. I'm riding to the Gavilan in a few minutes with Buck. I'll be back by sundown tomorrow. If you have any questions, Henry will tell you why. It's a peaceful trip. I won't even buckle on my rig.''

Turning to his mother, he said, ''Put a half dozen of those biscuits in a cloth for us, Mom. I don't want us riding into Gavilan with our ribs showing.''

An hour before suppertime the following evening Clayt appeared at the top of the trail and ''hallooed.'' Within minutes settlers began to appear, some wearing expectant expressions and others showing obvious concern.

By the time Clayt crossed the dam and turned the Gavilan chestnut loose in the corral, Henry had them assembled in the meeting house. Without wasting time on preliminaries, he turned the lectern over to Clayt.

Deliberately baiting their curiosity, Clayt regarded them with a serious face as he apparently searched for words. Even his mother, who used to say that she knew him very well— even before he was born—could not read his intention. Nelda and Kate with Oss between them, were equally puzzled. Henry refused to let himself guess the outcome. Jakob Gruen sat resigned to whatever the decision. He was a skilled artisan. He could work at his craft anywhere. San Francisco seemed attractive. John Bates privately bet on a sellout that would give him several thousand dollars. Mike Nathanson and Thad Jones, the most seriously wounded, could not move themselves from the edge of despair.

''I said I'd be back safely by sundown,'' Clayt began, ''and I am. When I rode down yesterday with Buck Tanner I did not know what to expect''—he paused—''and it's just as well that I didn't.''

An uneasy rustle ran through the room.

''I say 'just as well,' '' Clayt continued, ''because I could never have guessed what Tom Garner and Sir Charles were up to.''

He let them sit anxious on their seats for a long moment,

then without changing his tone or his expression, he said, "I can guarantee you that we will never again have anything to fear from the new owners because"—he paused again—"because, after a lot of learning from our friend Buck, you'll be looking at the new superintendent of the Gavilan."

Stunned, they sat in silence until the full import of the news began to sink in. Suddenly the big room was filled with exclamations of surprise and shouted questions.

Raising both hands, Clayt called, "Hold on! Hold on! There's a little more to tell!"

When the room quieted, he resumed his explanation.

"First of all, Buck Tanner is the new foreman." There was a burst of applause and pleased exclamations. Clayt waited for the reaction to subside. "He'll look after things and hire on new hands until I start in a week or so. They are going to pay me four hundred dollars a month and an overwrite on each head that is safely delivered to the railroad. I'm going to split that with Buck. He doesn't know that yet. Also, I will have my living and food."

The implication caused Mary to gasp quietly. If Clayt lived at the ranch, she would soon be alone, unless Kate could be persuaded to stay. Oss and Nelda would certainly marry now, as soon as the house was finished. With no more threat to the dam and the community, Henry would see to it that the men got back on the job as soon as possible. Only Kate greeted the news with no change of expression.

Later, at the supper table, when Clayt had supplied as many sensible answers as possible, Mary turned to Kate who had eaten in silence. "Well, at least until Nelda and Oss set up their own housekeeping, I'll have both of you here." She reached for Kate's hand. "I hope, dear, that you will consider this your home—as much yours as ours now. We feel that way, Kate. We love you like our own."

When Kate lowered her head and did not reply, Clayt spoke up from the head of the table.

"Mom means that, Kate. We all do. You're safe and welcome. You'll have everything you need."

Without lifting her eyes from hands clenched in her lap, her only response was a nod.

"By the way," Clayt added, "The buckskin mare is yours now. They wouldn't let me buy it...or the chestnut either. They are gifts from the owners—no strings."

Kate seemed to brighten a bit. She looked up. In a small voice she said, "I thank you, Clayt—and I thank them. Please say so."

As he got up, Clayt said, "Maybe you can tell them yourself one of these days." As he started to move away, he added, "And maybe you'd better get a name for her, too."

When the kitchen work was done, Kate left without saying goodnight and retired to the little storage room that had been fixed up for her. Carefully, she folded her few personal things. The new clothes that Oakley had sent Buck to buy for her were still at the ranch. Mary and Nelda had stitched some simple things together. These she folded—two plain dresses, two underskirts and drawers, and a cotton sleeping gown—and packed them in a flour sack pillowcase. A pair of huaraches and a pair of good slippers that Nelda had given her, she would put in the saddlebag together with a buckskin bag containing a brush and comb and some small tortoiseshell side combs that had belonged to Fern. When she had finished she concealed the lot under her bed and returned to the kitchen-living room.

"I think, if you'll excuse me," she said to Mary and Nelda, "I'm going to take some air and get to bed early."

Mary looked at her closely. "Do you feel alright, Kate? You seemed a little quiet and peaked at supper."

"I feel fine, thank you. I guess so much has happened in the last few days"—her shoulders bounced in a little shrug—"I'm a little tuckered out."

Mary continued to look at her closely for a bit longer, then smiled sympathetically. "I guess we all are. If we're not up when you come in, have a good night's rest."

Kate responded with a quiet, "Thank you," and returned to her room. For a time she sat on the edge of her bed, lost in a confusion of thoughts: She was welcome there. They all meant it. They were good people, so like her own. She did not want to leave them, but to stay knowing that Clayt would only be an occasional visitor, that he would be making the new life for himself that he had alluded to when he said he thought Red Creek and the settlement were becoming too confining, meant that he would be growing farther and farther away as he moved deeper and deeper into hard new work that she sensed he was well suited to.

There had been no man in her life before Clayt had saved her. Aside from her father's, his were the only arms to hold her. For some reason—and she had been aware of the terrifying possibility—the comancheros had not taken her to be used by the soldiers at Fort Sumner farther down the Pecos. The Apaches who had killed her family had turned her over to women in the tribe. She had been despised by the young women and abused with the most menial work, to be done on one poor meal a day. She was more dead than alive when the comancheros traded for her and, in its way, that could have been a blessing. Oakley had seen past her condition and had taken good care of her. Her own native strength and determination had brought about a remarkable improvement. Loving care at the Adams home had done the rest.

She knew that a good part of the hope that had grown and sustained her was the realization that she was falling in love. But as the weeks passed, during which Clayt was preoccupied with proving Harmer's guilt, his cold determination and so seldom seen evidence of gentleness and good humor discouraged her. The foolish hopes and desires that seemed so real in her fantasies grew more and more forlorn. When she tried to imagine a life without a man like Clayt, the prospect brought her to the brink of desperation and finally, now, to the act born of it.

With still enough light to make her way to the corral, Kate moved cautiously. If Clayt was down there, she did not want to risk being seen. He would ask questions that she would not, and could not, answer. Taking her time, she deliberately went out of her way to stop on the dam and watch the water sliding over the spillway. Here and there on the pond a late feeding fish splashed as it rose to take a careless insect from the surface. The night sounds were not in full chorus yet. She loved them. She had heard very little at Gavilan. There had been no time from the endless chores, no time free of the anxiety that had grown with each passing day. She drew in a deep breath and expelled it. Those unhappy certainties were behind her now, but she gladly faced these new uncertainties of her own making.

When it was full dark, she made her way to the tack shed to check the saddle and bridle. As she neared the corral the little buckskin mare trotted over and poked its nose between the rails. "Clayt said to give you a name," she whispered as she continued to caress the affectionate animal. "So... from now on you will be Molly. That was my mother's name—and she took good care of me, too."

Kate lingered outside until she saw the night lamp that had been left for her. Moving silently, she went to her room and stretched out. She dozed intermittently until she heard the first big barred rock rooster, then she gathered her things and slipped outside. In a matter of minutes she had saddled the buckskin, tied her belongings on the saddle strings and put her small things in the bags. Leading it through the gate, she closed it and walked the mare across the dam to the foot of the trail.

Mounting, she let the animal have her head in the waning darkness. At the top, she picked up the trail leading to the wagon road south. By the time she crossed the shallow ford on the Pecos, the sun's upper limb lit the sky with a reddish-orange fire. Its beauty made her catch her breath. Five minutes later she squinted against its brilliance as she attempted to follow the trail.

Knowing that she would be followed when she was missed, she continued toward the wagon road leading to Tres Dedos and the Gavilan. After a mile or so she doubled back to the west until she rejoined the Pecos. Deliberately, she chose a place where the mare could cross. In midstream, she doubled back again to shallow water, then kept the mare heading south so her tracks would be washed away. Continuing until she was opposite a dense stand of piñon and scrub oak, she left the shallows and rode into the cover to let the mare rest.

The first rays of the sun were beginning to slant down across the canyon rim when Mary Adams left her bedroom and entered the kitchen to poke up the coals and restart the fire in the big cast iron range.

Nelda, rubbing sleep from her eyes, joined her a few minutes later.

"I had trouble getting to sleep last night," she said. "I kept thinking about Clayt and what it's going to be like around here when he's down at the Gavilan most of the time."

Clayt heard her as he pushed open the door to his room. Shoving in his shirt tails as he walked, he came over and put his arms around his sister.

"You don't have to worry, Sis. Just keep in mind that I'll

be coming up here every few days just to make sure you hay shakers aren't stealing my water."

Nelda gave him a friendly shove. "Go on with you. You'll be coming up here to show off your new store-bought clothes."

"Not likely," he replied. "I'll be coming up here right after my first payday to divvy up some of the money I'll be stealing until I know what I'm doing. And right after that," he continued, "I'll be coming back to see the pretty new things you three bought in Las Vegas."

"Now quit funning," his mother said. "You know very well that Nelda and I will still be running up our own things, though I might just let the girls ride in to pick up some gingham and lace, and maybe one or two of those new patterns Ebenezer Butterick invented. I remember poor little Hilde bought several when they were still in New York. After she died Jakob brought one of them over but it was way too small. She was such a little thing." She laughed. "I guess you could say we'd be all dressed up and no place to go."

"Well, Mom, it's about time that changed." He looked at the stove. "I'll get the water this morning since we've got one sleepyhead."

Nelda stopped setting the table, a task she usually shared with Kate. "I haven't heard her stirring yet." She walked over and listened at the door then rapped lightly. When there was no response she turned to look at them. "That's funny. She's usually first one up." She rapped again then called.

When there was no answer she depressed the latch and opened the door a crack. For a moment she stood peering in, then she let out a startled little cry. "She's not here!" Opening the door wide enough to step in, she let out another little cry, "Her things are gone!"

The words were hardly out when Clayt pushed her aside. "What on earth has got into that girl?" he demanded. For a moment he stood undecided, then ran for the door, hesitated, then bolted for the corral. It took only seconds to determine that the buckskin mare was missing. He went in and out of the tack shed to double-check, then he ran to the house.

"That fool girl's gotten some crazy bee in her bonnet and taken off!"

"My Lord!" Mary exclaimed, "she probably feels she's not wanted now. She's said a dozen times that she's been feeling in the way. She's never really believed that she's as welcome as our own." She pressed her hands to her mouth as though to stifle the thought, then took Clayt by the arm. "Go look for her, for pity's sake! Where do you suppose she's gone?"

"Lord only knows!" Clayt replied, "But there's one place I'm sure she won't go!"

"The Gavilan?" Nelda asked.

"Right! If she's headed anywhere it will be into Las Vegas. As handy as she is, she could find work there."

"And God knows what else!" Mary whispered. "Go after her, Clayt. Find her and bring her back. Make her understand that she's loved and needed here!"

The thought of Kate Williams alone looking for work in Las Vegas which was rapidly gaining a reputation as bad as Dodge City's according to Mike Whittaker, angered and alarmed Clayt. If necessary he'd haul her back by that silly ponytail of hers and talk some sense into her head!

Clayt drove the big chestnut to the top of the trail at a pace that lathered the animal and had it wheezing. He slowed the pace as he picked up the fresh tracks. As it became clear that they were heading for the Pecos ford and the wagon road to Las Vegas, he pushed the animal again. At the ford there was still some moisture in the tracks.

Moving at a steady lope now, he followed them east until, for some reason he could not fathom, they turned back to the Pecos. When he splashed across and did not find tracks again he paused. Obviously, she expected to be followed. Doubling back it became clear that she had deliberately kept to the shallow water to obliterate her tracks. The question was, which way did she go? North, if she was going to Las Vegas. Staying to the shallows he rode until he came to a place where she would have been forced to leave the river. But she hadn't. He had guessed wrong. She was heading south. But that didn't make any sense. There was nothing down there but Tres Dedos and farther on, the Gavilan. She could bypass that in order not to be seen by Buck, but after that there was nothing. In time she'd cross the Pecos again when it turned southeast to meet the Gallinas.

Puzzled and both angry and worried, he took the chestnut to high ground along the river and spurred it into a fast gallop.

Several miles south of him, Kate had quit the cover of the piñon stand and taken to the road again. She would be missed for some time by now. Whether they would work or not, her plans were clear. And one thing was certain: she did not want them interfered with—especially by Clayton Adams—until they had a chance to work out.

From time to time she would turn in the saddle and scan the mesa behind her. If anybody was following she would know it by the dust and would have time to take cover again and hopefully avoid discovery. If it was Clayt following her that would take a miracle! The miracle might be managed at Tres Dedos if the Mexican would let her hide Molly. Forget it, she told herself. Her only chance was to avoid Clayt and whoever else was with him until they gave up. Time enough then to let them know why she had left. Silently, she called herself a fool for trying. That's what they'd call her, too, but it was too late for regrets. Too late, perhaps, to even think that she'd be forgiven.

When Clayt was opposite the point where he had lost Kate's tracks he began zigzagging toward the river and back to see if he could intercept them again. When he failed to find any fresh tracks on the wagon road anxiety and frustration turned to outspoken, cussed anger.

He rode on for another half hour before Kate saw his dust. In ten minutes he'd overtake her. Fighting desperation now born of her own acknowledged stupidity, Kate rode until she found a very dense stand of cover several hundred yards to the right of the road. She turned toward it. In a last effort to confuse them, she rode in tight circles to obliterate her tracks. Then she rode to the far side of the cover, dismounted, and tried to scuff out the hoofprints. Cattle had been loafing in the cover. That might help.

She had been at it for only a few minutes when she could make out for certain that her pursuer was alone. It was Clayt on the big chestnut. Resigned, she mounted the buckskin mare and waited. If the confusion of tracks worked she still might manage to take cover in one of the deep barrancas that veined the mesa until he rode on.

Sooner than she expected, Clayt reined up and studied the ground. After several minutes he turned the chestnut to the left and appeared to be riding off to the east. Relieved, Kate took hope again but it was short lived when she realized that he was riding in ever widening circles. If he continued, it was only a matter of minutes before he'd pick up her poorly scuffed tracks leading to her cover. After the third circle, Clayt was within a hundred yards or so of the thick stand of piñon and scrub oak. She watched him rein up and look around, study the tracks some more then, to her complete dismay, he turned the proud-cut chestnut directly toward her hiding place.

Before she could think of an explanation, the little buckskin, tossed its head and let out a welcoming whinny.

Kate's shoulders slumped. "Oh, Molly! Oh, Molly!" she moaned. "It was too much to ask you to save my neck twice."

The words were scarcely out when Clayt came crashing through the cover. Shielding his face from the limbs, he reined up to a brace-legged stop.

"What the devil do you think you're doing?" he demanded. "Who are you hiding from—and why?"

Feeling guilty and stupid, Kate had no recourse but to brazen it out. "I'm hiding from you, Clayton Adams—and why is none of your business!"

"You're running away—and that *is* my business!"

"I'm not running away. I'm leaving for a very good reason!"

"And just where do you think you're going?"

"If you must know, I'm going to the Gavilan."

Unable to believe his ears, Clayt all but shouted.

"The Gavilan! You're out of your mind! And just what do you think you're going to do there?" he demanded.

Kate thrust her chin out and stiffened her back.

"I may be out of my mind, but I'm going there to see that the new superintendent of the Gavilan does not live in a pigpen!"

Clayt's mouth flew open. For an instant he stared at her in disbelief. Then, for the first time in years, he gave in to uninhibited laughter.

Forcing the chestnut close, he reached over for the mare's bridle.

"Get down off that buckskin, you sassy brat!"

Before she had time to react, Clayt was off the horse lifting her bodily from the saddle. Planting her on the ground facing him, he took her by the shoulders and glared at her in mock severity.

"You're not going to do a thing for the new superintendent of the Gavilan—or anywhere else, young lady—so long as folks have to call you *Miss* Williams!''

When Kate's defiance melted into tears, Clayt brought her close and snugged her cheek against his chest. After a time, she eased away and looked up at him.

''I hate girls who blubber,'' she said in a small voice, ''but I went and fell in love with you—and I didn't know a better way to tell you.''

Clayt nodded. ''I know, little Kate,'' he said gently. ''Lately, I've been having the same trouble.''